The

Dismantled

Minds

First edition published in 2025
© Copyright 2025
Allison Osborne

The right of Allison Osborne to be identified as the author of this work has been asserted by her in accordance with the Copyright, Designs and Patents Act 1998.

All rights reserved. No reproduction, copy or transmission of this publication may be made without express prior written permission. No paragraph of this publication may be reproduced, copied or transmitted except with express prior written permission or in accordance with the provisions of the Copyright Act 1956 (as amended). Any person who commits any unauthorised act in relation to this publication may be liable to criminal prosecution and civil claims for damage.

All characters appearing in this work are fictitious. Any resemblance to real persons, living or dead, is purely coincidental. The opinions expressed herein are those of the author and not of Orange Pip Books.

Paperback ISBN: 978-1-80424-666-5
ePub ISBN: 978-1-80424-667-2
PDF ISBN: 978-1-80424-668-9

Published by Orange Pip Books
335 Princess Park Manor, Royal Drive,
London, N11 3GX
www.orangepipbooks.com

Holmes & Co. Mysteries

Collection one
The Introduction of Holmes & Co
A Study in Victory Red
The Circle Code Conundrum
The Impossible Murderer
The Happy Family Facade
The Red Rover Society
The Detective's Nemesis

Collection Two
The Adventures of Holmes & Co
The Hidden Case
The Missing Two
The American Visitors
The Dismantled Minds
The French Translator
Return to Baskerville

What object is served by this circle of misery and violence and fear?

-Sherlock Holmes, *The Adventure of the Cardboard Box*

Chapter I

An Incident Outside the Butcher's

Irene Holmes stood on her tiptoes to see over the queue to the butcher's shop, sighing at the dozen people still in front.

"I simply abhor lines." She placed a hand on her hat to keep it in place as a gust of wind blew. "They make good practice for observations, however, they are rather tedious."

Doctor Joe Watson stood beside her, clutching a full bag of books from his trip to the booksellers down the street. "It's the least we can do for Miss Hudson; considering the reason her knees are so worn is that she takes care of us."

"Oh, I know." Irene kicked at a stone on the ground as the sleeves of her cream blouse flapped in yet another gust. "I just wish I could create some type of diversion so we could hop up a few places."

"Please do not anger this butcher." Joe adjusted his vest – an exact, yet unplanned colour match to Irene's trousers. "We already have to avoid the baker on Talbot because you insulted the way they kept their milk."

"It was inadequate!"

She had lectured the baker on the process of the cow and milking, which had earned her and Joe permanent banishment from the bakery.

"If only we'd brought Isla." Irene sighed again, thinking of their West Highland Terrier probably having a lovely nap in front of the fire.

"And have her growl at everyone?" Joe laughed. "She's getting better, though I wish she wouldn't pick up social cues from you. I swear you birthed her the way she eyes everyone around her like they might have dangerous secrets."

"Everyone *does* has dangerous secrets."

The queue moved up, causing the pair to shuffle forward. Joe rubbed his face, to which Irene quirked her eyebrow.

"You are tired and sullen despite just purchasing books. You are worried about something. One would assume it's an issue with Sarah, however, she is out of town, and you've seemed quite relaxed since she left – which is wholly another matter that I am sure you're contemplating. Regardless, your eyes are crinkling every minute; your gaze has yet to settle upon anything for longer than ten seconds. You also keep tapping your fingers against your leg and it's not Morse code or any pattern I can figure out."

Her friend ran his fingers through his auburn hair, the strands so long they began to curl over the tops of his ears. "It is both comforting and frightening that you pay so close attention to me."

"You are easy to observe."

He shrugged and gestured to the streets of London. "There is a lot going on, I suppose."

Irene glanced at their surroundings as well, noting the queue and the pedestrians on the pavement. "Correct. Cheating spouse. Pregnant. Two kids. Three dogs. Works full time in an office... Do you want a story for each of them?"

Joe chuckled. "I meant to do with me. And Baker Street. Us."

The line moved again.

"Oh." Irene pursed her lips. "Well, all of that is fairly simple."

"Is it?"

"Yes. We have to get the materials to wrap Miss Hudson's garden before the cold weather descends; plus there is a shutter that needs replacing. And this winter we *will* be using the coal man to bring our sacks right up the stairs. Neither one of us needs to be carrying it, as we have more important things to do. And I will *not* be spending another winter cooped up in the flat, so we will seek out cases if we have to."

Joe switched his bag of books to his other hand. "Perhaps you're right."

She raised her brow at him, hands on her hips.

He rolled his eyes. "Of *course* you're right."

"I always am."

He made a noise that suggested that she was not, in fact, always right.

As Irene turned with a retort on her tongue, a deep cry of surprise came from down the street. Then others, exclaiming in shock.

All Irene could see was a large delivery truck parked by the grocers. She went to step out of line, but Joe grabbed her shoulder.

"Miss Hudson will kill us if we don't get this meat."

A crowd gathered around the truck; someone shouted for an ambulance.

Irene looked at him as more cries came.

He released her. "Alright, let's go."

She hurried through the crowd, pushing people to see the scene.

The truck had stopped next to the store, the driver at the rear. A young woman, barely over eighteen, stumbled around the pavement, confused and groaning as she tried to get her bearings. She wore a frayed, dusty brown skirt, her tan blouse was covered in dirt, and a dark brown substance dotted her shoulders.

Dried blood.

Her filthy bare feet captured Irene's attention, as did her stringy hair that looked like it had fallen out in clumps.

The woman paused to shake her head, pressing her palms into her eyes. Spotting Irene in the crowd, she stumbled forward, arms outstretched, fingers twitching. Her mouth opened and closed as if she were desperate to speak but couldn't figure out how. Up close, the woman's cheeks were gaunt, and her eyes were glassy and distant.

The crowd behind Irene gasped and shuffled backwards, but she stayed put. This woman was frightened, but not dangerous.

Behind them, the truck driver paced, wringing a hat in his hands.

"She fell out the back when I stopped to unload," he said, voice shaking. "No idea where she came from, I swear."

Joe caught up to her and towered over the two women. "We need to get her off the street or else this will cause an even bigger scene."

Irene spotted a tailor shop a building down and turned to the driver. "Wait here for Scotland Yard. Joe, come." She held out her arms, as if herding cattle, to get the woman's attention again. "This way."

The woman's body needed a moment to catch up to the instructions. Irene moved closer as the crowd continued to gather.

The woman walked forward, right into Irene, and as soon as they touched, she grabbed on to her, moaning again.

"You are safe," Irene tried. "Now, this way."

She moved them forward toward the tailor's. When they made it inside the shop, the woman behind the counter gasped.

"Ring for an ambulance right now. We need to borrow your dressing rooms."

Irene kept moving all the way to the small room with a curtain at the back. The girl stumbled and fell onto a cushion.

Joe had followed, now clutching his bag of books to his chest. "She's shivering."

The girl went to move, but Irene touched her shoulder.

"No. Stay there. You're safe now."

Moving slowly, the girl pressed her hand against her chest and then showed two fingers.

"Two?" Irene guessed. "Two what?"

Again, she struck her own collarbone and held up two fingers.

"Number two. You are number two?"

The woman nodded, tears welling in her eyes again.

Irene turned to Joe. "Ring Eddy. Then get that driver's information – name and business. Find out what stops he made since loading his truck, and when he stopped at each. Something foul and terrible has happened to this poor woman, and I fear the worst."

"What's the worst?"

"That there are more."

* * * * *

It didn't take long for two medics to reach the tailor's. As they both entered the small back room, though, the young woman squirmed away. She kept her head down, shaking.

"It is safe," Irene tried when the girl gripped her sleeve. "We must go with them. It is to help you." The woman didn't move. Irene looked at the paramedics. "I will ride in the back with her."

Thankfully, they didn't argue, instead leading the two out of the building and back onto the pavement. Joe still stood with the truck driver in the middle of a heated conversation.

"But I have deliveries to make."

"Those are not my orders," Joe said, voice stern and commanding. "They are from Scotland Yard."

The driver mumbled, but leaned on his truck.

"Joe," Irene called. "Meet us at the hospital."

He gave her a nod.

Irene climbed into the vehicle and beckoned her frazzled companion. Slowly and reluctantly, the girl climbed inside, cowering on the floor as if the walls were closing in on her.

Her demeanour stayed the same for the entire journey to the hospital. Taking minutes to register what was right in front of her, arms curled around her knees.

"Come," Irene called as they reached their destination. Simple words and phrases appeared to work; the girl obeyed yet still clung to Irene's arm.

Irene got her to sit in a wheelchair. Despite her dislike of lifts, she held on to the handles of the chair as the box ascended.

Sitting on something other than a hard stool – or the back of a truck – must've been comfortable enough because the young woman almost fell asleep.

They made it into an empty private room, Irene shushing people and glaring at nurses as they went. A paramedic trailed behind her, doing his best to explain the situation. She parked the wheelchair inside a vacant room, lightly shaking the woman awake.

"On there, please," she said, indicating the bed.

The girl stared, eyes wide with fear.

"It's safe." Irene sat on the bed and bounced on the hard mattress a few times. "See? Please lay down."

She was reluctant and clearly distraught, but still laid onto the bed in a curled ball.

The door behind opened, and the nurse gasped.

"Oh my..."

This disturbance rattled the girl, and she whimpered.

"It's okay," Irene said, holding her hand. "This nice nurse is here to help you."

Staying near the doorway, the nurse gave a nod to Irene. Just as the girl settled, Joe entered the room.

"He is a friend, too," Irene said quickly. "He helped me when we found you. He is an animal doctor. He helps them feel better. He is good. He can stay."

Irene stroked Joe's arm as the girl stared at him. The man stood stock still, clutching his bag of books once again.

The young woman eventually relaxed.

"I'll go into the corner," Joe mumbled. "Lestrade is on his way."

Irene gave the nurse a signal to approach while remaining in the girl's steel grip. She'd never been in contact with so many people in one day. It unnerved her. Even she and Eddy didn't hug as often. She didn't mind Joe's touch, however. In fact, she needed it in her life, as he was the only person whose touch she appreciated.

As the nurse approached the bed with a medical cart, the girl moaned and nearly tumbled to the floor. Her glazed eyes were still wide and feral.

The nurse froze. "We need to examine her."

"You will," Irene said. "Give her a minute."

Five minutes passed in strained silence, the girl staring at the cart, chest rising and falling in heaps.

Irene took matters into her own hands. "I don't see any deep wounds or anything. Take that away."

"We will need her in a gown," the nurse protested. "Those clothes will not due; they smell something foul and are scratching up her skin."

"Agreed. I will help put the gown on."

Again, the nurse didn't argue, for which Irene was grateful. Most nurses she'd met were capable and had proven themselves during the mess of the war; she was glad that this nurse was one of the good ones. The ones who knew better than to question her.

Irene held the hospital gown out. "We're going to dress you in this to look at you. Do you understand?"

The girl slowly touched the robe, nodding.

The door behind them opened, bringing in the doctor. His long white coat swished as he strode into the middle of the room.

Upon seeing him, the young woman made a horrible, gut-wrenching howl and slid to the floor, curling tight into a ball.

Irene flung her hand up. "Leave the room."

"I need to examine her."

"Clearly you aren't getting anywhere near her." Irene restrained herself, but just barely. "The nurse and I are handling it. Please leave before you send her into fits."

The man didn't move, though. She let out a purposeful sigh.

"If you wish to argue, fine. You may take it up with the Detective Inspector on his way over. Regardless, leave the room."

Joe shuffled forward, either to further Irene's point, or to stop her from lunging at the doctor should he make any smart remarks.

The nurse folded her arms, standing firm as well.

The doctor finally waved them off and exited.

Joe resumed his place in the corner while Irene coaxed the girl back into bed. Feeling safer, she climbed back onto the mattress.

With the nurse's help, they got the dirty clothes off. Irene folded the brown skirt and blouse neatly, placing them on the table for later examination.

"Still has undergarments on," she said. "No rips or tears."

"A relief." The nurse looked at Irene, probably thinking the same thing: she still had her dignity intact as far as they could tell.

There were no other harsh marks on her body, no lacerations or severe bruising. Just small, fresh dark spots from bouncing around in the back of the truck.

"Clean body," Irene narrated to Joe as he scribbled notes.

As the nurse tugged the gown on, Irene gently examined the girl's hands.

"Garden dirt." She scraped the dark, rich soil from under the girls' nail beds. "Ripped fingernails."

They were jagged and rough, two scratched down to the cuticle. This woman had climbed and clawed her way out of some place secured by a wooden door.

The nurse stayed next to Irene, but out of her way as she continued to look at the girl, who had finally relaxed. While her body had been relatively bruise free, her wrists and ankles were darkened with angry purple and yellow splotches.

"Wrists and ankles were shackled," Irene continued. "With rope, not metal."

That caused the girl to shiver.

"I'll get her blankets," the nurse said, before leaving the room.

In the meantime, Irene couldn't help the soft smile on her face. Joe had faced the wall for the whole process, jotting notes down in his book. Doctor Watson and his heart of gold.

Sensing her eyes on him, he spoke. "Is the examine finished?"

"Not quite. I'm giving her a break while the nurse returns. You may turn around, though."

"This poor girl."

Irene nodded. "But pity won't solve the case any faster. I have a few more things to examine, and Eddy still needs to get here for his statement, but then she needs to eat and rest."

The nurse returned, and they wrapped the girl up.

"Open your mouth for me, please." Irene said.

As the woman parted her lips, Irene noted perfect teeth in need of a simple brushing. Her tongue was still intact and there was no swelling, meaning her mutism was psychological.

"Joe, hand me your pen and a blank page." He did as asked, and she held it out for the girl. "Can you write your name?"

The girl stared. She drew a straight line, then squinted at it. She tried again, but never got further than another line.

Irene took the book and pen back. "You can understand me, correct?"

She nodded.

"Do you remember the name of the man that you escaped from?"

The woman stared at her with a blank expression.

"The man's name," Irene tried again.

The young woman shook her head, stringy hair dangling.

"Do you remember anything of where you were held?"

Looking up, the girl shuddered and hunched her shoulders.

"Something above you," Irene said. "Something scary and bad."

Tears formed in her eyes. She nodded as a droplet escaped. A knock came from the door and Eddy slipping quietly inside.

The girl reacted fast, and Irene immediately stepped in.

"He is a friend. A Detective Inspector. Police. He is here to help, I promise. He will not hurt you or touch you. He simply needs to write what I tell him to."

Irene put her hand on her friend's tall shoulder, then hugged his arm. Eddy stood still with a soft smile on his face, attempting to seem harmless.

The girl calmed, trusting Irene completely now. She released Eddy and stepped back to the bedside.

"Will she provide a statement?" he asked softly.

Irene shook her head. "Her ability to speak has been taken from her."

"Taken?"

Nodding, Irene started on the final piece to her puzzle. She peeled back the thin bit of hair covering the girl's ear. A small, scabbed hole sat in her temple, bruising all round, blending into her greying skin. Irene moved to the other side of her head: the same hole, but messier and more bruised.

Irene gave another quick once over. Glazed eyes. Sluggish demeanour with bouts of jerkiness. Muteness. Memory loss.

Her stomach dropped, which surprised her as she never reacted physically to anything else she'd come across.

Perhaps this time was an exception.

Perhaps because it was matters of the brain.

She turned to look at Eddy, the nurse, and Joe. "This woman has been lobotomised."

Chapter II
The Victim's Identity

Joe stared at Irene, ensuring he heard her correctly. "Lobotomised?"

His friend nodded, keeping her gaze on the woman. He underlined and circled the word in his notes.

He'd obviously heard of the practise of drilling into the side of the head to scramble the brain, but he'd never witnessed the effects. It was done to sedate or control a person, as well as treat mental disorders.

The harsh-lit hospital room was already unnerving enough, with the pale thin woman who could do nothing but moan, yet the image turned his stomach.

In the back, Lestrade also looked paler than usual. Joe knew the DI had seen some dark things during his career, but this walking ghost seemed to give him pause as well.

"She was kept in a basement," Irene continued, pulling Joe back to the case. "The man who did this was solely after the lobotomy, as there's no indication of foul play anywhere else on her body."

Joe continued jotting his notes, relieved that this woman – though terrorised – had been spared other horrors.

His partner continued speaking to the nurse, who'd more than graciously took orders from someone with no medical qualifications. "Thank you for your help. We'll let her rest now. I want only you to check on her and ring us should anything new happen. Allow no visitors. If someone turns up, refuse them entrance, even if they state they are friends or relatives."

The nurse nodded. "I'll attempt to bathe her, but I won't push. Luckily, I'm just starting my shift, and perhaps I'll stay extra hours. Lord knows I could use the pay, and this girl could use some consistency."

"That would be most excellent of you. Two constables will be posted out in the hall. Let them do the heavy work should someone try to come in. And do not let any doctor visit. At all."

"No one in here but me, Miss Holmes. I promise."

Irene turned to the young girl. "You will eat, and you will rest. The nurse will wash you. We will be back later."

The woman nodded.

In a turn of uncharacteristic events, Irene turned back to the nurse and stuck her hand out. "Thank you."

The nurse shook her hand. "I saw a lot through the war, but this is beyond strange and dark. I promise, however, she is in good care."

Closing his book, Joe made a mental note to praise Irene later. She was still snappy and curt, but offering a thanks and praise of her own volition to someone else was very rare and should be encouraged. He'd been worried at first that her approach to the poor girl would be too harsh and serious, but the woman had responded well to blunt, simple orders. A side effect of a scrambled brain, he supposed. They could only pray it would get better.

Of course, Joe knew very little about brains and lobotomies, but he was about to acquire more knowledge than he bargained for.

Lestrade stayed back, presumably to give the nurse his telephone number should she need it, as the pair filed out of the hospital room. When he finally joined them, he let out a long sigh.

"This will not be a fun one."

Joe nodded in agreement.

Irene, however, was on fire, pacing back and forth, gaze bouncing everywhere.

As Lestrade opened his mouth to speak, the erratic private detective whirled to him. "If you have any constables that are young and kind, post them outside the room."

"Great minds think alike. I have two who are as non-threatening as they come."

Joe fiddled with the strap on his bag, stomach still uneasy. "You believe she's in danger?"

Irene shrugged. "I'm not sure yet, but I don't want to take a chance. How would the man that did this to her act if he gains access to the hospital? Try to take her back? Try to finish this operation if he deemed it unsuccessful? Attempt to end her life? Possibly all of the above."

Lestrade frowned. "Most likely, he will try to take her back to wherever he kept her."

Joe peered beyond the DI to the hospital room. "She wouldn't go back with her captor, would she?"

Irene paused her pacing. "Fear can paralyse someone. Make them revert to when they were kidnapped. She may think she has no choice. He may convince her, using whatever tactic he employed when he originally captured her."

"I will order the doctor to stay away," Lestrade said. "And search for the identity of this girl. I'll ring you when I've discovered anything."

"As expected."

The DI pointed at her. "This is a very serious case, Irene. The main reason you are being kept on is because this woman trusts you. But this *is* a serious police matter, and it will be treated as such. Whoever this man is, he is dangerous."

"We've dealt with dangerous before."

"I know, and it got poor Joe shot and kidnapped. And did you forget about your fight in the cinema lavatory mere months ago?"

Joe winced at the memory; Irene, in a dress that cost more than their flat, tussling with a madwoman, hell-bent on seeking revenge on an actress she thought killed her husband. His friend's legs had been cut up by a shattered ashtray, her temple split.

To his surprise, Irene didn't snap back or roll her eyes at all.

"I understand."

"Good. Go back to Baker Street, wash up, and wait for me to ring."

* * * * *

The front foyer of 221 Baker Street was a welcome sight. While Joe didn't have a particular fear of hospitals, the scene today turned him off the entire doctor-patient setting for the foreseeable future. They'd have to go back at some point, but hopefully next time he'd be better prepared.

"Joseph Watson and Irene Holmes!" Miss Hudson's angry Scottish brogue snap. "It's about bloody time you got back! I need—" The older woman stopped short. "Where are the groceries?!"

Irene waved her off. "We found a case!"

"At the butchers? Was it 'who did the cow in'? Because even I could tell you it was the damn butcher!"

Isla barked from the top of the stairs. Irene hurried up to meet her, leaving Joe in the older woman's wrath.

"A young woman was wandering around the pavement. She was…" He trailed off, wondering how to put the issue gently. He didn't get a chance though, because Irene yelled down from the top of the sitars.

"Her head was drilled into, and her brain was scrambled."

Miss Hudson looked at Joe, horror in her eyes.

"Well, then. I'll put the kettle on."

Joe headed upstairs, book bag heavy in his hands. The dog flew out of the flat and danced at his feet until he scratched her ears.

Irene was sorting through the mail as he entered the sitting area. Joe set his new pile of reading material on his side table.

Irene thrust a letter into his face. "Who's Annette?"

He straightened, taking the envelope. "Wasn't she the girl from the finishing school that was so keen on helping us?"

Irene furrowed her brow and went to the couch. She must've remembered how many people she'd touched the past few hours because she stopped herself, wobbling on her heels before snapping upright.

"Ah yes. Read it aloud, if you please."

He wasn't sure if she remembered Annette, but he read the letter, anyway. "Dear Miss Holmes and Doctor Watson. Hopefully you remember me, as I haven't forgotten either of you in the least. I am finished with my schooling and am not sure quite what to do with myself. Would your business require an assistant or secretary? If so, I would gladly apply for that position. I would even work for free as an apprentice to gain experience."

He forwent reading the sign-off as Irene never cared about those, before folding the letter and sticking it back inside the envelope.

"Certainly interesting. Some cases could've used an extra set of hands."

Irene stood in the middle of the room with her arms crossed and a brow raised. "What shall we do? Place a secretary desk in the hallway? At the bottom of the stairs?"

Joe set the letter down on the small table beside his armchair, an amused smile on his lips. In his mind, however, he conjured up an image of an office where each of them had their own desk, with a secretary taking telephone calls and organising all their papers. They'd have several boards for their clues and an entire wall of textbooks for research. The images came so easily that he had to drag himself back to Baker Street before he got carried away.

Luckily, Miss Hudson entered with toasted tomato sandwiches.

"Ah, Miss Hudson," Irene said. "I require hot water for the bath. I have touched too many people today and I wish to scrub them off."

The landlady stared at her. "Why were you touching so many people? You don't even hug *me* when I ask."

"It was for the purpose of a case. Now, I am feeling itchy, and if I think too much about it, I will begin to squirm and may vomit. A bath, please."

* * * * *

Within the hour, splashes came from the lavatory as Irene washed. Joe had taken Isla out and settled in his chair to review his notes from the hospital. Reading over the word lobotomy, underlined and circled, gave him chills. The description of the poor girl wasn't any better. He closed his book, knowing he wouldn't gain any insight reliving the horrors.

He caught sight of Annette's letter.

"Shall I write the girl back?" He called.

"You may," Irene yelled back. "I'm not sure what to say to her, though."

"Perhaps I will wait, then. We can discuss it after the case."

The telephone rang and Joe pulled himself up, tossing the letter back on the table. "Joe Watson speaking."

"Joe, Ed here."

"Your voice doesn't sound promising."

"No, everything is fine." The DI sighed as if everything was not quite fine. "I feel this case is going to be tough and we don't have many answers yet. Anyway, I found out who our victim is. Nettie Lawson. Her parents are on their way to the hospital. They were quite beside themselves when I told them I'd found their daughter and I tried to prepare them for the worst, but they wouldn't have it. They were too elated to have her back alive."

"Regardless of her state," Joe said, "a daughter alive is better than a daughter dead."

A loud crash came from the lavatory and the door banged open.

Oblivious, Lestrade continued. "Quite right. Look, tell Irene to be gentle when you both arrive. The parents sound posh and might not take too kindly to her forward attitude."

The scents of orange and lemon puffed around the room.

"I will do my best. See you soon, Ed."

He set the receiver down as Irene called from behind him.

"Was that Eddy? What happened?" She stumbled out of the lavatory, wrapped in his robe.

Joe didn't answer at first as he took the chaos in. Irene's hair was dry and pinned to her head, but water ran down from the robe off her bare feet and collected on the carpet, seeping into the floor.

He'd seen her in a robe before – and with her hair messed up – but this was like scenes he'd read in books that turned way too intimate for his liking.

"That was Lestrade," he stammered. "He found our victim. The girl's name is Nettie, and her parents are on their way to the hospital."

"Ah, wonderful news! We shall hurry up there. I would like to witness her reaction to seeing them and if that will reveal anything."

Joe distracted himself by scratching Isla's ears. "Surely the girl's parents wouldn't have sent her to get lobotomised?"

"That is what I want to observe."

Miss Hudson entered the room and immediately gasped. "Oh, good heavens, Irene! If you are going to parade around like that, then you better plan on proposing to the poor doctor. This kind of dress is only appropriate in front of a husband."

Irene snorted. "I was in fewer clothes at that film premiere a month ago."

Joe stayed crouched, petting the dog, letting the women battle it out.

"Go get dressed." Miss Hudson shooed her away. "I have to dry this floor now. How much soap did you use? Good *heavens*."

Joe stood in time to see Irene roll her eyes. She stomped away to her bedroom, shutting the door.

As they waited for her to get dressed, Joe stood on towels with Miss Hudson to dry up the water. After a few minutes, the landlady muttered something about fetching more towels and hurried away.

Irene emerged in dark trousers and a matching dark shirt, with Joe's robe in her hands. She tossed it to him before scooping her hat from the hook. "I'm ready. I shall see you down at the car."

Joe sighed.

His robe was soaked, and the smell of lemon and orange was so strong that he doubted he'd ever get it out of the fabric.

* * * * *

Joe and Irene made it to the hospital before Nettie's parents did, as they were coming in from out of town.

They waited in the hallway for only a minute before a very frazzled older couple rushed toward the room. Though they were in a hurry, the pair had an air about them. From the woman's dress to the man's suit, they radiated luxury.

Joe led Irene a few steps away to give the parents some privacy, and though she tried to tug away to get a front row view, she obliged, and they moved to the other side of the hall.

Lestrade stopped the parents briefly, confirming their identity, before allowing them into the room.

The girl – Nettie – looked clean now, but her skin was still sallow and malnourished. Her hair was pinned off her face, though the nurse left a few pieces loose to cover the drill holes.

She looked up when her parents entered the room. Although it took a moment, her lips stretched into a smile and she made happy groaning noises.

Her parents ran to her bedside, sobbing.

It was the most emotion Irene and Joe had seen from Nettie, but her reactions were subdued.

Irene went right up to the window, observing as if at a zoo. Joe's instinct was to tug her away again to give the family some privacy, but he let her have a minute. It wouldn't take her long to observe what she needed.

After a moment, Nettie's mother caught sight of Irene. She started crying all over again and rushed from the room, swiftly wrapping her in a hug.

Irene stiffened, keeping her arms at her sides. Her face looked as if she'd swallowed a lemon.

Joe held out his hands to help his friend, but it was too late.

Mrs. Lawson sobbed and repeatedly thanked Irene.

After an eternity, the woman finally released her and she shuffled back toward Joe, taking shelter at his side. She cleared her throat before speaking. "Mrs. Lawson. We'd like to ask you a few questions."

The woman wasn't listening. She'd turned back to gaze at her daughter.

Her husband, eyes red and puffy, stepped out as well. "We can answer anything you need," he responded instead of his wife, having overheard. "Anything at all."

"Excellent. We—"

Joe cut Irene off, grasping her shoulders. "We'll give you a few more minutes. When you're ready, we'll speak on those chairs over there."

Mr. Lawson nodded gratefully and joined his wife and daughter in the room once more.

Irene went rigid under Joe's touch, but he knew it was out of stubbornness than discomfort.

"Give them a minute," he hissed in her ear. "You'll get your information. Let's go sit down."

"I just don't understand. They have their daughter back. She isn't going anywhere. Why can't they answer my questions right now?"

They made it to a pair of chairs in the small waiting area.

"When you've lost something, sometimes you want to hold on to it once found, in case it goes missing again."

"I suppose." Irene folded her arms, slumping in the seat. "I just hope they can shed some light on how their daughter went missing in the first place."

"Let's hope they can."

Chapter III

A Sister's Tall Tale

Fortunately, Mr. and Mrs. Lawson didn't take too long to join Irene, Joe, and Eddy in the small waiting area.

"Tell us about her," Eddy started. "Her age—"

"When did you discover Nettie missing?" Irene cut in and she felt Eddy stiffen beside her, but she ignored it. He wasn't asking the right questions. At least not yet. The girl's age was unimportant right now.

Mrs. Lawson looked from Eddy to Irene. "At the beginning of spring. March seventh. She and her sister, Marg, were visiting a friend up north near Surrey. Marg said Nettie met a man in a pub and ran off with him."

Eddy went to speak, but he was too slow.

"Did she offer any description of this man?" Irene pressed.

"Young and handsome was all she said. It would seem that Nettie was smitten with him right away. It never made much sense, as our girl was already being courted by a lovely young man named Geoff. We thought she was quite taken by him, and were surprised when we heard she'd run off with someone else. But now we know that wasn't the case…"

Mrs. Lawson erupted into a sobbing mess.

Eddy produced a handkerchief for the woman.

While it was sad to see the state of this poor mother, Irene needed to get on with the questioning. "You were given no indication of where Nettie had gone, other than word from her sister?"

Mr. Lawson patted his wife's shoulder, then nodded. "That's correct. No letter or anything, which is even more odd. Nettie loves to write."

His last sentence struck a sad chord inside Irene. The image of the shaky line that the young woman produced earlier in the day flashed in her mind. She tried to shake the empathy as it didn't help at this particular moment, but it stuck with her.

She opened her mouth to ask something, anything, pertaining to this case to keep her thoughts distracted from spiralling with the empathy, but Eddy beat her to it.

"Does this sister have an address? We would like to speak with her. Or have you contacted her, and she is on her way here as well?"

Irene straightened, cheeks warming at being caught off guard by her own woes.

"Her address would be helpful," she said, catching the curious sideways glance from Joe. He shifted his weight so his knee was touching hers in a move she recognized as comforting. She almost moved her leg away, annoyed at herself for clearly displaying some type of distress.

Mrs. Lawson had her crying under control and looked at her husband.

They both hesitated, but eventually, Mr. Lawson spoke.

"This is rather embarrassing, if I may admit," he said, eyes welling with tears. "And I am even more ashamed that I didn't push Marg for more information."

"Please get to the answer," Irene urged.

"We're not sure where she lives," Mrs. Lawson said, voice meek. "She moved in with some girlfriends when Nettie went missing, and she asked us not to visit. She was devastated. We know the neighbourhood, but we've respected her wishes as we didn't want to lose her either. She will send us the occasional letter—"

"Do you have a letter you can get to us as quick as possible?"

Mr. Lawson kept his head down, as if trying to compose himself. His wife, though, reached into her purse and produced an envelope. "We met the postman as we were leaving the house."

Irene grabbed the letter a bit too quick. She flipped it over and over, examining the heavy, expensive paper and flowery handwriting. It had been dropped and stepped on by a size 6 shoe that had recently trod in fresh dirt.

She stood.

"Give Doctor Watson the name of the neighbourhood. And be gentle with Nettie. She can neither speak nor write and it would frustrate her if you encouraged her to do so at this moment. If she does happen to remember anything about her captor – even the smallest detail – or any new information comes to light, please ring us at the telephone number my colleague will leave with you."

She stepped away, striding down the hall toward the exit, needing to keep her momentum going. Her mind wandering into sad and dark territory had scared her, the tremor that used to shake her hand threatened to return.

Eddy's heavy shoes hurried behind her. "Irene, wait. Please stop."

She spun to the DI, gripping the letter tight as if he might pluck it from her hands.

"You may find the house," he said. "But you will wait until I arrive before conducting any sort of interview."

"Yes, yes."

"Promise?"

She folded her arms. "We will not speak to the sister without your presence."

"Jolly good. Find the house and wait. I will be there after I collect my own statement from the parents."

"Fine." She went to spin around to continue on her way, but Eddy held her arm.

"Are you alright?"

"I am." She softened her voice in an attempt to convey that she truly was fine, at least in this moment. She never really hid her feelings from him, but the hospital was not the place to bare her soul.

Eddy narrowed his eyes, but he released her arm. "I'll see you at Marg's house."

* * * * *

Irene drove slowly through a neighbourhood on the south side of London. People came home from work in automobiles or walking from the bus stops. Meanwhile, she and Joe were on the lookout for a garden with freshly turned dirt and pavement that was recently done or had been worked on in the past week.

Joe tapped on the window. "What about that one?"

Irene slowed the vehicle. The dirt was roughened as if plants were removed for the winter, and the pavement was covered in dust from a small garden wall being constructed at the neighbouring house.

"Ah, ha! Joe, I think you've done it. Now, we wait for Eddy."

She turned the car around and parked it up the street so the house was still visible. They hadn't waited for ten minutes before the door opened and a young woman strolled out, purse in hand.

"I do believe that is Marg," Irene said. A man appeared from inside the house and fixed something on the hinges before shutting the door.

"That doesn't look like the few girlfriends she's supposed to be living with, however," Joe remarked.

"It most certainly does not."

Irene reached for the door handle, but Joe stretched and grabbed her wrist. "No. We told Lestrade we would wait for him."

She wiggled under his grasp, but his long slim arm was surprisingly strong.

"We told him we wouldn't speak to *Marg* without him. I want to find out who this man is."

"Even more of a reason to wait for the police."

"It will be fine, Joe. I'll pretend the automobile has broken down or something. I will figure it out." She slowly wrapped her fingers around the door handle.

"And should he look out to see me sitting in the car?"

"I simply won't let him look!"

With that, she flung the door open and jumped out.

Joe grabbed for her, but she had gotten away and out onto the road.

"Irene, don't—"

All she needed was a quick conversation with this mystery man. She didn't think he was the perpetrator, as he had yet to take Marg anywhere and seemed to be playing house currently. Perhaps, if she asked the right questions, she could find out more information than if Eddy interrogated him.

She rapped loudly on the door. The man answered with a pleasant smile. He was young, and objectively handsome, with broad shoulders and dark eyes. But they were downturned and tired, and he stood with a hitch in his hip, as if injured during the war.

"Yes?"

"Hello. My automobile has broken down. May I use your telephone to ring someone to help me?"

"Oh dear!" The man peeked out the door. "That yours at the end of the road there?"

"Yes."

"I can take a look at it for you."

"That's quite alright. I'll ring my husband and he'll be right out."

Irene paid careful attention to his reaction. If this was a man who would take advantage of women, then surely he would object, or some facial muscle would twitch.

Instead, he nodded and stepped back. "Of course. Come right in."

"Thank you." She entered the small foyer.

"The telephone is just in the hallway there."

The man stepped past her and headed into a small reading room to the right, to a desk filled with papers.

Irene took her time wandering down the hallway, looking at the photos hanging on the wall. A few pictures of him and Marg were strewn about, but not one of Nettie. People removed photos of family if they were grieving – she'd even done it herself – but it still struck her as odd.

She found a wedding photo that appeared very recent, showing Marg with a full smile on her face.

The man stuck his head out of the sitting room. "Everything alright?"

"Oh, yes," Irene replied, realising she'd stared at the photos for longer than she meant. She pointed at one. "Your wife's dress is lovely. When were you wed?"

"Recently. Last month."

"Ah, well congratulations."

He smiled at her compliment, but the expression was hollow and practised.

And sad.

"Thank you."

"I'll make my telephone call and be on my way."

"Are you sure you don't want me to take a look at the automobile for you?"

She waved the offer off. "No need. I'll be out of your hair in a moment."

Marg's husband nodded and went back into the sitting room.

Irene pretended to dial a number and talk to her imaginary husband for a moment, before hanging up. She popped her head into the sitting room.

"All jolly good. Thank you…" She trailed off, asking for his name.

"Geoff. And it was no trouble at all."

"Geoff," she repeated. "Take care."

A familiar rush of adrenaline surged through her. This man was Nettie's former boyfriend. Geoff – who was now married to her sister – was clearly still in mourning.

So, how did he and Marg ended up married?

Theories bombarded Irene as she headed out. Did he marry Marg because she reminded him of Nettie? Did Marg have more to do with Nettie's kidnapping than simply seeing her walk away with another man? Irene doubted this man had anything to do with it, as he seemed sad to simply exist, but perhaps he was sad because he *was* involved with it.

She wanted to ask Geoff a million questions, but she knew to wait for Eddy. Her DI friend would already be quite furious at her for entering the house without his permission, but to give out information about the case – and such a serious dark matter too – was something not even Irene would mess with.

At least not now, with her respect for her friend's career rising over the past year.

She was nearly to the car, still tucked half behind a wall at the end of the street, when she spotted Marg out of the corner of her eye, carrying bread in a paper bag.

Irene hurried her steps toward the car. As she approached, though, the nose of a Wolseley stuck out behind the Vauxhall.

"Oh drats."

Eddy leaned against the driver's door, arms folded and shoulders stiff, his small dark eyes fixed on her.

Joe stood beside him, looking at Irene with a raised brow.

"Before you get upset—"

The DI cut her off. "Too late. I am tempted to bar you from the rest of this case, Irene Holmes, and I still might."

"No, Eddy, listen! Marg doesn't live with girlfriends. She lives with and is married to Geoff, Nettie's former beau."

"Good lord."

"See, that's why I—"

He held up his hand. "Right now, we are going to march back into that house and interview the sister. You are coming with us only because this is a sensitive subject, and a woman present might get me better answers. But you will keep your mouth shut. Is that clear?"

Irene's stomach tightened with guilt, and she looked at the ground. She was about to argue that at least she hadn't spoken to Geoff about Nettie, but she just nodded.

"Wonderful. Let's go."

She trudged behind the two men as they went up to the house. Eddy gave a sharp knock.

Geoff answered the door and spotted Irene instantly.

"Hello again! Do you still need help with your car?"

"Please disregard her," Eddy said. "I'm DI Lestrade and we're here to speak with you and Marg."

Geoff stepped back, calling to his wife as he did so.

Within five minutes, the kettle was on and the five of them sat in the small sitting room. Joe and Eddy took up the couch, Marg and Geoff sat in opposite chairs, and Irene stood behind the couch. Eddy had denied her a seat, clearly punishing her for moving ahead without them. She didn't mind at all, as she could observe the entire conversation and everyone's expressions better.

"Your sister, Nettie," Eddy began, "was found alive. She is currently in hospital being treated for some horrific injuries."

His words hung in the air for a moment before Marg made a squeaking noise and burst into tears. "She's alive?"

"What happened to her?" Geoff asked, face lighting up. "Where did you find her? What hospital is she at?"

Marg's tears weren't fake, but Irene couldn't tell if the woman was overjoyed that her sister was alive, or because of her husband's eagerness.

Eddy held his hand up. "We won't give that information out yet, for her safety. Nor can I go into much more detail. But I need to ask some questions."

Geoff pointed at Irene. "Who are *you*, then? Did your car really break down?"

"She is a liaison and assisting with this case," Eddy interjected.

Irene needed to get a question in. Her friend would eventually get to all of the information, but there were certain things she needed to ask because sometimes a person's reaction gave more information than the answer themselves.

As the DI paused to dig out his notebook, she pounced. "Your parents informed us that you claimed Nettie left willingly with a strange man at the pub. Is this true? Or was it a lie you told to steal her boyfriend? Did she go with that man willingly, or was she was taken from the pub?"

Joe gave her a stern look over his shoulder. Eddy, on the other hand, resembled a boiling kettle.

"She left with him!" Marg cried, then spun to her husband. "I swear! She left."

"On her own accord?" Irene snapped.

"Yes," the sister stammered.

Irene swallowed a triumphant grin. "She didn't. She wasn't forced, but it wasn't entirely on her own free will. Explain."

Geoff pulled away from his wife, eyes wide.

The woman kept sobbing.

Irene heaved a long, frustrated breath. She leaned forward over the couch and snapped her fingers right in the girl's face. "You may cry all you want later. We need more details if we are to find who did this to your sister and prevent him from doing this to other women."

The girl wiped her face and nodded.

"Okay. Sorry. I'm so sorry. My parents are going to hate me so much."

"You can deal with that later. Where were you when your sister went off with another man? Are you able to tell us the entire story without tears interrupting the narrative?"

"I can try."

"I need you to *do*. Not try."

Marg started bawling all over again, causing Irene to roll her eyes.

Eddy hissed something to Joe, who stood and hurried around the couch, grabbing Irene's arm. Before she could react, he had dragged her out into the front hallway.

She stumbled after him, but his grip held. "Let me go."

"Not until you settle down."

He released her at the front door. Irene tried skirting around him, but Joe grabbed her waist and gently pinned her against the wall. His body was centimetres off hers and she stared hard into his shoulder, willing this mountain of flesh and bone to move.

"Please stay here for a minute," Joe said softly. "You are being too harsh."

Irene continued to glare at his sweater vest.

The conversation in the sitting room carried to them. Eddy must've decided to continue with Irene's interrogation, because he urged the girl to speak about what happened.

Joe stayed in front of Irene and she tried to calm herself, at least until he let her go back into the room.

She heard Marg start her tale. "Nettie loved travelling to the small towns outside of London. Said it was her mission to visit them all. And she used to drive her own car, going alone. Something about it being quieter that way and enabling her to think straight."

The sister paused.

Irene looked up at Joe. Sometimes, if she looked at him just right, he would fold and let her do anything. She had yet to figure out exactly how to reproduce that look, as she never knew she was doing it in the first place, but it was worth the try now.

Joe sighed and shuffled to the side. He caught her though, before she moved forward, his arm around her waist again.

"Let Ed do the talking or else I will drag you outside to the car."

A stirring in her stomach arose, either frustration or some other emotion, but she conceded nonetheless.

He released her, and the two returned to the room for the rest of the tale.

Geoff stared at the ground, face red. Marg, in turn, wrung her hands and spoke as if he wasn't sitting right next to her.

"She was with Geoff, but he loved her so much more than she ever loved him. I was the one who loved him. I could give him the life he wanted. Not her, who wanted to be on her own."

The man hung his head even further, but didn't interfere.

"One day Nettie said she was travelling to this small town outside Surrey. I paid a cabby a lot of pounds to follow her to the town and I saw her go into a pub. When I looked, she was just sitting by herself in the corner, reading." Marg huffed. "She went all that way to read a book? It didn't make any sense to me. Then a man approached her—"

"Can you describe him, please?" Eddy interrupted.

"Tall, but kind of hunched over. He had nice hair – dark, almost black – and was kind of handsome from what I could see. He spoke to her, and Nettie laughed flirtatiously. So, the man sat down with her for a few minutes, then they got up and left together. I was out of money by then, so the cabby took me home. I was so mad because I thought she was leaving Geoff to be with that stranger. I didn't tell anyone what I saw for the same reason. But then she never returned. The guilt was almost not worth it. But then Geoff and I found each other, so maybe it was worth—"

"Nothing was worth letting your sister wander off with a strange man, never to be seen again." Irene bit out. "Certainly not a fiancé who is only with you, so he can still be a part of the family should Nettie ever return."

"I… No…"

Not listening, Irene rounded on Geoff. "Why did you not write to her parents to tell them you two were married?"

He finally looked up, eyes red – an empty shell of the man who'd greeted her earlier. "She convinced me that they were too heartbroken and wanted nothing to do with us anymore. I'm sorry… I need a minute…"

He stood, but Marg grabbed his arm. "No, darling, please stay. I can explain."

Shaking his head, he looked at Eddy. "I'll gladly answer any other questions once you are done with her. I will be in the office down the hall, then at my brother's – I will provide the address."

Eddy let the man go as Marg erupted into another crying fit.

Irene was done. Marg couldn't offer any more information; she was now simply a pathetic sight to watch.

"I suggest you get yourself to the hospital. I do believe your parents will be furious and you may lose a husband. Good day."

She pivoted on her heel and marched out of the house, letting the front door slam behind her.

Chapter IV

A New Addition to the Team

"Go," Lestrade said to Joe. "I'll finish up here and meet you at the car."

He nodded and hurried to where Irene paced by the Vauxhall, her hands clenched.

"What happened in there? Are you alright?"

"Am *I* alright? Is *she*? Letting her sister get kidnapped by a madman and then lying about it? I've seen some heinous things in my time, but this... I despise people like that. People with no loyalty."

For a moment, Joe was at a loss for words. Irene never put this much stock into strangers, so there had to be something deeper. He placed a hand on her shoulder.

"I understand. But I've never seen you get this riled up over something I would assume seems so trivial and almost annoying to you."

Irene shrugged. "Love turns people into such foolish beings. I've said it time and time again."

He squeezed her shoulder again. "Ah, it's love you have the issue with."

"I'm hungry. And I feel we will need to take a long drive out to Surrey at some point."

Joe meant to respond, whether to agree or to call out her avoidance, but Lestrade jogged to meet them then.

"You've upset her good, Irene."

She wiggled out of Joe's grasp and folded her arms, leaning back on the car and continuing to glare at the ground.

Lestrade turned his attention to Joe instead. "I'm going to Scotland Yard to transcribe these notes, then back to the hospital to see if any progress has been made and check on Nettie. I will ring you if anything has changed."

"We'll find out what's around Surrey and why Nettie would've been drawn to it," Joe said. "Perhaps take a drive and ask around, save you the time in case something else happens at the hospital."

"That would be grand, Doctor. Thank you."

They shook hands, and Lestrade turned to Irene.

"This case is bothering you more than others."

She wrapped her arms around herself. "Minds are delicate and shouldn't be scrambled."

The DI stared at her for a few seconds before drawing his friend into a one-armed hug. "Talk to me or to Joe if you need to. Understood?"

Irene still pouted but didn't resist the affection. Lestrade released her, and she climbed into the driver's seat of the Vauxhall.

"I'll keep an eye on her," Joe reassured. "And I'll do my best to restrain her should she attempt to go rogue."

This pulled a smile from the DI. "Good luck with that."

They shook hands and Lestrade retreated to his own automobile.

As Joe slid into the passenger seat, Irene started the engine. She stared out the windshield, shooting bullets with her gaze.

He'd finally made the connection from her anger to the reason. Sherlock had lost his mind – the thing he was most known for. Of course Irene would be sensitive on this topic, but it never occurred to Joe just how much it would affect her. They'd seen many terrible things during their cases; some that he thought would hit close to home for her but were easily brushed off.

A sensitive Irene made for a snappy and cruel woman who put up a shield to deflect and defend to keep people away.

And they were dealing with delicate people who wouldn't take too kindly to her attitude, nor would it get them far in the case.

As they drove back to Baker Street, Joe reached out and took his partner's hand. She gave a squeeze back. Neither one of them spoke about the case for the entire journey.

* * * * *

Irene paused at the door to yawn. She didn't bother to cover her mouth, which caused Joe to yawn. He, however, covered his mouth, then waved his hand to hurry her through the door. He was starving and needed to use the lavatory. If Irene needed to as well, she gave no indication as she trudged over the threshold. He squeezed past her.

As he burst through the door to 221b, Miss Hudson greeted him. "Ah, welcome home, Love. I just put out these sandwiches."

He paused and eyed the plate, debating if his trip to the lavatory could wait until after he filled his stomach.

Irene entered and spotted the food immediately.

"Oh, lovely." She said flatly, grabbing two off the plate. She went into her bedroom and shut the door behind her.

Miss Hudson looked at Joe. "Check on her before you go up to your room, will you? I feel like if I ask her if she's okay, she'll say yes and brush me off."

"Will do, Miss Hudson."

"Goodnight, Hen."

She left the room and Joe sighed, eyeing the lavatory once more. He knew he should check on Irene in case she fell asleep and forgot to eat, or any of the other myriad of scenarios that could happen in the time he was in the loo.

He took a big bite of a sandwich, then knocked on her door.

"Not now, Miss Hudson."

"It's Joe."

"Oh."

He didn't know if that was an invitation, but he opened the door, anyway. Irene sat on her bed, staring at her two sandwiches.

"They're good," he said. "You should eat. It was a long day."

"Yes. I will."

"Are you okay?"

She looked up at him with those dark eyes of hers and nodded. "Yes. Well, I will be. I always am in the end. Just all this talk of scrambled brains and taking family for granted has frustratingly touched a nerve, so I must wait it out, then send it away."

She plucked a sandwich from the plate and poked at the bread. Joe had two choices: either sit with her, force her to eat, and pry at her feelings, or step away and trust that she'd listen to him.

At least, those used to be his choices. He'd learnt over the past six months or so that there was a time and place for each of his reactions. Just because Irene expressed herself in extremes didn't mean Joe always had to reciprocate. Sometimes an acknowledgement was enough to either get her to open up or to feel a bit better.

"Good job," he said softly.

She raised a brow. "For…?"

"For recognising your feelings and being open about them."

"You sound like a psychologist."

"I *am* a doctor." He winked, earning a smile from her; or rather, an annoyed smirk.

"Of animals."

"Still a doctor. Eat your sandwich. I'll see you tomorrow."

Joe stepped out of her room and heard Irene call just before he shut the door. "Thank you."

The sincerity in her voice made him smile.

"You're welcome."

He shoved the rest of his sandwich into his mouth and headed to the lavatory.

As melancholy as Irene was tonight, she'd be back to her spry self tomorrow.

* * * * *

The following early morning found both Joe and Irene dressed and at the little dining table, awaiting breakfast. Just as he predicted, his partner was as alert as ever, fingers tapping the wood in anticipation.

Just then, the landlady sauntered in with some plates.

"Potatoes and eggs. No bacon."

While Miss Hudson understood why they didn't bring home any meat from the butcher's, she had stated that it threw all her meal plans into complete disarray and that they'd need to wait until she could get some fresh meat today.

Irene didn't seem bothered as she dug into her eggs, neither did Joe, who had gone months without meat in his lifetime.

Just as they finished their meal, the front doorbell rang.

A light, lovely voice drifted upstairs and for a moment Joe panicked. It sounded like Sarah, and she wasn't due back from her trip for another day or two. Not that it would matter if she was home early, as there was a part of Joe that missed her. Unfortunately, and for reasons he had yet to sort through, there was a bigger part of him that was glad for the break from having to plan dates.

As Miss Hudson led the guest up the stairs, it was apparent that it wasn't Sarah, but a new woman entirely.

Joe felt guilt swirl in his stomach, yet stood to greet whomever was about to walk through the door.

Irene stood as well and hopped over the couch to her armchair, as if she was the queen awaiting an audience, leaving her dirty plate on the table.

The newcomer had dark blonde hair, cut short and curled, and she was dressed in an expensive-looking coat and hat, with matching gloves.

She seemed familiar to Joe, but he couldn't quite place her.

"This is Annette," Miss Hudson introduced. "She's come here about a job."

"Well, um, actually," the lady started, wringing her hands nervously. "I was wondering if you got my letter and if you needed any help with…anything?"

Of course, this was the young woman from the finishing school who'd written them a letter earlier in the week… Actually, it had just been yesterday since they'd received her letter. So much had happened in so little time.

"Ah yes. Pleased to meet you. We did receive your letter, um…" He hesitated, unsure of how to approach this.

Miss Hudson ushered the girl to sit, then hurried off to make tea.

Before anyone could start a conversation, the telephone rang.

Joe jumped to grab the receiver. "Hello?"

"Hey Doc. Ed here." There was a pregnant pause before he continued. "Another girl was found. Same clothes, same dirt and bruises. Except she's apparently got two wicked black eyes, and only the start of a drill mark. Better get to the hospital in case we need Irene to talk to this one, too."

"We'll meet you there."

Joe hung up the phone and turned to the two women, who both stared at him with excited intensity.

"Another girl—"

Irene jumped from her chair. "Eddy is on his way?"

"Yes."

"Good. We will beat him there, but that is no matter." She turned to Annette. "Do you get queasy easily?"

"Oh, uh, no, not at all."

"You can take notes and transcribe them well?"

"I know shorthand and am quick with a pen and a typewriter."

"Can you drive a vehicle?"

"Yes, though I am out of practice."

"Can you keep your thoughts to yourself unless prompted?"

"Of course."

"Can you regulate your emotions and reactions?"

Annette giggled. "One lesson we're taught at the school is how to remain poise under any circumstance."

"Excellent," Irene said. You may come along and observe. I cannot pay you for this case, as we are assisting the police and not taking on a client of our own, but you may use it to see if you would like to help us in the future."

Annette's eyes widened and a grin spread over her pretty face. "Oh, Miss Holmes, that would be wonderful! Thank you. I didn't bring a notebook or anything."

Irene grabbed her hat. Isla danced around at her feet, excited by the activity. "Simply observe this visit. And if you want to keep observing this case, you may find any notebook of your choosing. You didn't drive here, so you will ride with us, but if things should work out, we may need to get you an automobile of your own."

"Understood. And, had I known I'd be travelling with you, I would've worn something matching as well."

Joe looked at Irene. They both wore dark dusty blue today with brown shoes. He'd all but given up attempting *not* to match with her. Sometimes, he'd change his outfit at the last minute, attempting to trick the universe, but he would always emerge in the same colours as his partner.

Irene looked at Joe. "*Oh*, we do match. Don't worry about it. We do not do it on purpose. Now, onwards."

Annette nodded, her head bobbing up and down in excitement. "Yes. Thank you, Miss Holmes. I really mean it."

Irene strode by her and headed toward the door. "Wait to thank me until you've seen what we've been dealing with."

That didn't quell the girl's excitement as she followed Irene out the door.

Joe gave Isla a scratch. Irene was only allowed on this case because the victims would speak to her, and now she was bringing on another person... Lestrade would have both their heads.

Either Annette would be a blessing to have around, or he'd end up babysitting not one, but *two* over-eager women.

* * * * *

The hospital had placed the second victim in the room directly next to Nettie's, which was up a few floors. Annette had aimed toward the lift, but quickly changed direction when Joe and Irene headed toward the staircase.

"Is there a reason we don't take lifts?" The young woman asked, her heels clip—clopping opposite Irene's and making all sorts of echoes in the stairwell. "Is this to check for possible bad guys that might hide in here?"

"No. It is because we do not trust lifts."

"Oh."

Hearing the reasoning out loud warmed Joe's cheeks in embarrassment. It did sound silly; lifts would most likely be in every building in London in a few years' time.

Undisturbed, Irene pushed through the door to their target floor.

DI Thom Gregory was there when they arrived. Clad in a charcoal grey suit with shiny shoes, he gave the trio a cool wave as they approached.

"I assume Eddy has filled you in," Irene said, trying to see around him into the room.

"Yes. I answered the call about this victim and knew he was working the case, so I rang him as soon as I got here with her."

"So, why are you still here?"

Joe let out an audible sigh. "Irene…"

But Gregory simply chuckled. "Because the last time you worked a case without me, it turned out to be with American film stars. I am not missing out again. Though this one seems much darker."

Joe frowned. "Sadly, yes. This is the second victim?"

The DI nodded. "She didn't fall off the back of a truck like the last one, though. Instead, she was found wandering the streets just outside of the city. According to the nurse, this girl seems much more lucid than the first." Gregory spotted Annette and smoothed his hair, flashing her a grin. "Hello there."

Irene had stepped away toward the room, so Joe made the introductions. "Annette, this is DI Gregory. Gregory, this is Annette, our assistant on this case."

Gregory grasped her hand gently. "Call me Thom, sweetheart."

The girl giggled. "Nice to meet you."

"Leave her, Thom," Irene called. "I need her focused to know if she is going to work out or not."

He winked at Annette, then stepped aside. "Ed said I could let you in, so long as you didn't upset her. Said you had a rapport with the other girl."

"Correct." She opened the door to the room slowly, Annette at her heels.

Joe stood at the door so he could see in the room, but could quickly step back if needed.

The same nurse who had tended to Nettie moved around the bed, fluffing the pillow and covering the girl's shoulders. Irene stepped up beside the bed, giving Joe a full view of this second victim.

While psychologically more alert than Nettie, she looked worse for wear. Heavy black bruises outlined her eyes, and her cheeks were pale and gaunt. She still had her hair, but it was clipped short and jagged.

"Hello. My name is Irene Holmes. This is my colleague, Dr. Watson, and our assistant, Annette—"

As the young assistant got a better look at the girl, she gasped and covered her mouth.

"Lizzie?!"

Chapter V
The Second Girl

Familiarity swirled in Irene's mind. The appearance of this young woman and the name Lizzie attempted to form a connection but didn't quite touch. Annette said her name again, and finally, the memory came to Irene.

Lizzie Robert. The second missing girl from their case earlier in the year. The girl they'd dismissed as safe after her parents had received a letter stating that she'd met a man and had married.

Lizzie's parents had been nonchalant about their daughter's disappearance and had contacted Irene and Joe as an afterthought when they'd received the letter from her. The finishing school that Lizzie attended was situated just outside of Surrey, where these kidnappings had taken place.

Theories swirled inside Irene's mind. She felt the gears turning and her brain steaming forward with thoughts. A new gusto entered her, and she spun to Annette to give her orders and ask questions all at once.

The young woman was in tears, kneeling on the bed in front of her former classmate. "Lizzie, oh my god. What happened?"

Lizzie simply stared at Annette, as if her mind was slowly processing who she was. Finally, her dull, glassy eyes widened among the bruises. She made a sad, groaning noise and reached out her arms. Annette hugged her gingerly, then climbed off the bed, wrapping her arms around herself, as if afraid to touch anything else.

"What happened to her?"

"She was lobotomised," Irene said. "Are you going to be of help with this case? Or would you like to go home?"

She recognised the harshness, but the sight of Lizzie had surprised even her. As terrible as it was seeing a former classmate in this state, she needed everyone on this case focused.

Dead bodies were certainly easier to stomach than bruised and battered women.

Annette wiped her face. "I am fine. I promise."

"Good." Irene then turned to the nurse. "Similar bruising to Nettie?"

"Wrists and ankles. Undergarments are still on, no sign of any other trauma."

Lizzie perked up. "Neh… Neh…"

She tried to speak, but it was as if she couldn't remember how to finish her thoughts. "Neh… Neh…"

"Nettie?" Irene said. "Are you trying to say Nettie?"

The young girl nodded.

Irene spun to Joe. "Fetch a wheelchair."

Annette, who luckily caught on to Irene's idea, urged Lizzie from the bed. They moved her easily into the wheelchair Joe procured. Irene wheeled the girl to the next room, banging the door open harder than she meant to.

Nettie slowly sat up at the commotion. Her colour was much better today, and with her clean skin and washed hair, she now simply looked malnourished, rather than a victim.

Lizzie and Nettie stared at one another for a long moment before Lizzie broke the silence. "Neh! Neh!"

She still didn't get the full name out, but she leaned forward, reaching toward the girl in the bed. It took Nettie a bit longer, but she made a similar squeaking sound and shimmied to the side of the bed.

The girls met halfway, Lizzie climbing up on the mattress. They held each other and cried, though the second girl's face stayed dry, her tear ducts ruined by whatever had been inflicted upon her.

Annette cried as well, softer this time.

Irene's stomach churned as she watched these two young women, beaten and bruised, clinging to each other as if they were family. Their shared ordeal had forged a strong bond between them.

Beside her, Annette sniffled. "That was nice of you."

"There was a purpose," Irene said. "They were held together. It was obvious at first, but this indicates they got to know one another wherever they were. Perhaps they escaped together, or helped one another."

Her mind played the roster of people she had unwillingly bonded to because of trauma. Jeannie and her girls, all of them hiding in a bomb shelter, hugging one another, praying that the explosions missed them. Eddy sticking by her side when her father's mind deteriorated, and when Uncle John died.

Even Joe. In the almost two years they'd been friends, they'd both received their share of injuries and difficult cases and became all that much closer for it.

Annette sniffled again, and Irene looked at her.

"Sorry," she mumbled.

"Empathy is good," Irene said, feeling a lump in her own throat. "It means you care. You just have to know when to turn it off for the sake of solving a case."

"How do you do it?"

"Sometimes I don't turn it on in the first place." She pivoted away from the girls, who gestured to each other and tried to have a conversation. "Give them a few more minutes, then Lizzie has to go back to her room to rest. You may join them if you wish, but do not ask them any questions, as I want to be present for any answers they may give. Simply observe them and let them comfort one another."

Annette nodded and joined the girls.

Irene stepped back with Joe. He gently wrapped his arm around her shoulder, and they left the room to join Thom in the hallway.

* * * * *

They eventually got Lizzie back to her room and into bed. She seemed exhausted, but somehow content.

Eddy showed up just as Lizzie settled. She didn't seem as frightened of men as Nettie, and Irene couldn't tell if it was because she hadn't been held captive as long, or because she was more aware of who Joe and Eddy were.

Still, both men kept their distance.

Thom stayed well back, which struck Irene as curious. She'd never known the DI to shy away from anything grotesque, and yet, he was unable to look at the women for more than a minute or so. For all his cockiness and desire to solve cases better than Eddy, he had a soft heart.

Of course, the sight of these women would jar anyone who looked at them, as proven by Irene herself, stomach flipping every time she looked at Lizzie and Nettie. Regardless, she needed to press on.

She stood in Lizzie's room with Annette, ready to question the new victim, hoping she could respond better than Nettie could.

"Do you remember where you were taken to?"

Lizzie thought for a moment, then made a triangle with her hands above her head.

"A house. The basement of a house."

She paused, then nodded. "Dow. Dow. Col…" She wrapped her arms around her and mimicked shivering.

"Cold," Irene repeated. "Cold in the basement. A cellar."

Lizzie nodded again.

"Were there any other women there? Or just you and Nettie."

She stared hard at the bed, then jabbed a finger into her chest. She pointed at the wall separating hers and Nettie's room, then held up two fingers.

"Just two of you."

Another nod.

"You ran away with Charlotte many months ago, right?"

This question stumped her, and she tilted her head like a dog, dark eyes narrowing amongst the bruises.

"A long time ago," Irene tried again. "You ran away to a pub. You met a man there. Yes?"

Lizzie nodded, though her brows furrowed slightly.

"You did not know this man. But you went away with him."

The girl's lip quivered, and she nodded, hanging her head low.

"Was this house he took you to close to the pub?"

She pondered the question, then nodded.

"Did he speak about any other women? Or girls he had done this procedure on before?"

Lizzie winced. She shook her head, her gaze turning frantic. She made noises sounding like the word 'hat'. Her fingers wiggled, as if she wanted something in them.

Irene spun to Joe. "Notebook."

He opened to a blank page and handed the book and his pen over. She, in turn, gave them to Lizzie.

Lizzie bunched over the page, drawing lines on the paper. Most of them looked like the letter 'J'. She drew the letter repeatedly, more frustrated every time until the page was full. Just as Irene was about to take the book from her, the girl threw it to the bed and let out a mournful sigh. She buried her face in her hands and cried.

Irene took the book and handed it back to Joe.

Annette stepped in and immediately comforted Lizzie. "It's alright. You did so well." She patted the girl on the shoulders and pulled the blanket back over her.

Irene stepped out into the hallway with Joe and the two DIs while Annette tucked Lizzie in. "He'll be on the hunt now. With two surgeries done, and his patients escaped, he'll most likely be looking for his next victim. We must move fast to find him."

"A house just outside of Surrey," Thom said. "That could be anywhere."

"There are ways to tell."

"I know," the DI responded flatly. "I was making a general statement."

"Well, that's neither helpful nor productive."

Annette joined them in the hall, her eyes red but dry.

Eddy continued the conversation, taking command of the group. "Before I got the call about Lizzie, I was checking for victims who had died from lobotomies. I'd only just begun, so I will continue that."

"I'll contact Lizzie's family," Thom said. "Now that we know who she is."

"Collect the letter she sent them," Irene said. "Apparently, she'd written to them telling of her engagement as her reason for running off. The parents may still have it as a form of sentimentality."

He nodded. "I certainly like these visits better than telling a family their loved one is injured or dead."

He stuck his hat on and headed down the hall behind Eddy.

"As for us," Irene said to Joe and Annette. "We will—"

"Go to Scotland Yard as well?" Annette cut her off, clearly excited at the mere prospect of travelling downtown.

"No," Irene said. She was trying her best not to be too blunt to the young woman, but if Annette wanted to be their assistant, she had to learn, and this was the only way Irene knew how to teach. "We will go to the library. Much of our work is sitting and researching and thinking. The excitement is limited."

Joe snorted. "I wish that were true."

"Do you go on many adventures with your cases?"

Irene shot a glare at Joe. While she had hope for Annette after seeing how she handled Lizzie, she knew that the girl's job would mostly be note-taking and waiting for Eddy or Thom to call them, should she even want to continue working with them. Irene certainly didn't want her gallivanting around with her and Joe, as three was simply too large of a company.

Also, she didn't want the girl to get hurt. She had to keep remembering that their cases *were* dangerous, and Annette was at risk should she stay with them.

"We do what we must to solve our cases," Irene said, deciding on a bit of harsh words to put the matter to bed. "But your job is note-taking and observing. Understood?"

Annette nodded. "Yes. Of course."

"Good. Now, to the library."

* * * * *

Though it was an unusually warm autumn in London, the wind carried a chill.

Irene had sent Annette ahead to secure them a table in the library's records and newsprints section. By the time she and Joe made it to the first step, the young woman was up and through the doors.

As they started up the library steps themselves, Irene asked something that flitted across her mind every so often. "When does

Sarah return from her trip? She was away, wasn't she? Or are we going to see her inside?"

Joe shook his head. "She doesn't work here anymore. She got an office job as a typist."

"Good for her, I suppose. You don't speak about her much and I couldn't remember if you told me she was away on a trip or if you'd ended the relationship."

Joe stopped halfway up the steps. "Do you think I should?"

Irene turned to look at him. "Should what? Speak about her more? Not really."

"No, I meant… Never mind. Let's discuss something else."

Irene raised a brow. She hadn't pushed a button to irritate him, but he didn't want to talk about his relationship with Sarah. Unless she was reading him completely wrong, which she doubted. Of course, he was hard to read when it came to Sarah because his words contradicted his actions.

He squirmed under her gaze. "Annette is already in the building. Let's catch up."

She dropped the subject for now and jogged to catch him.

"Speaking of Annette. Have you observed how attached she is to Eddy?"

Joe threw his head back and laughed and the tension releases from his shoulders. "Ah, now we are gossiping. I forgot that you do love a good gossip."

Her lips spread in a smile. "A good gossip, yes. Informative chit chat, even better. Her infatuation with Eddy was so obvious it was hardly worth mentioning. Though, I will say that despite the age difference, it could work out in both their favours."

"I've never seen him interested in anyone, lady or otherwise."

"This is true. Perhaps he hasn't found the right person. Or perhaps he is satisfied with no one but friends."

Joe laughed again. "Oh, I cannot wait to tell Miss Hudson how you gossiped about your friend's love life. She'll invite you to tea with the ladies."

Irene snorted. "The day I go to tea with the ladies is the day *I* get a lobotomy."

He grabbed her arm and dragged her to him, hissing in her ear between laughs. "Irene. Not funny."

She squeezed his arm in return. "A wee bit funny."

They both giggled like children in trouble. Irene held on to her friend until they made it to the stairs to the second floor. He'd been very wary of her touches toward him recently because of a request from Sarah, but he seemed to have forgotten all about it while she was out of town. So, Irene took every opportunity she could.

Inside, Annette waved to them from the second floor, and bounced eagerly as they approached. "So, what now?"

"We sit and we research," Irene said, heading to the big boxes of newsprints.

* * * * *

A few hours – and a hundred papers – later, Irene had grown frustrated. Joe had tackled the medical papers, discovering many works written about lobotomy procedures. The most common one – a drill to the temples – was used on Nettie. However, their culprit used a new procedure on Lizzie – ice picks through her tear ducts.

Irene's stomach turned as she listened to the effects of lobotomies. How could simply reading about these things make her stomach flip like a flapjack?

She knew, of course. Her father's mind and cures for memory loss bounced around her head each time she picked up another article. And with each line she read, each bit of information Joe told her, her ribs squeezed into her lungs and she dug her fingernails into her palms.

She said nothing out loud to Joe, but at one point, where she was sure her palms were bleeding from her nails, her friend gently squeezed her shoulder.

He glanced at her fists, then back into her eyes. She released her hands, stretching her fingers and relaxing. He let her go, and she almost asked for his hand back.

They all returned to their articles, but it wasn't too long before Joe exclaimed. "Ah ha! I found something."

He skimmed the paper, picking out the important details as he'd become accustomed to, which Irene could not be more grateful for.

"A French man was arrested in London just before the war broke out. He was performing illegal lobotomies for a hefty price. According to this, there was no trial; he was apparently sent back to France for execution. It doesn't mention if he got there or not."

"Oh," Annette said. "That's a coincidence, so that must be our culprit?"

Irene shook her head. "There are no coincidences. We cannot say for sure if this is our culprit until we exhaust the facts. A good thing to note."

"Oh right, sorry."

"Don't be sorry. Simply learn."

Annette nodded like an obedient pup.

All of Irene's worries dropped off like a heavy coat as she focused on this new lead. "We'll go to Scotland Yard and see if Eddy or Thom can reach out to the French police for records of this man."

She stood and grabbed the paper, tucking it under her arm.

As she walked away, she heard Annette ask, "Are you allowed to take the papers out of the library?"

To which Joe sighed. "No, you're not."

Chapter VI

A Very Full Office in Scotland Yard

Joe led the way through Scotland Yard toward the back offices as Irene followed right on his heels. Annette trailed behind them, smiling at every constable who looked her way.

Usually, the attention they received was due to Irene and the interest in whatever case they were working on. Now, with Annette and her gracious manners and cute, bouncy walk, the main floor flooded with constables all trying to have a gander at Joe and Irene's new colleague. Joe saw a few slink away and knew that behind him, Irene was shooting daggers.

They finally reached the office and Joe gave a light knock on the propped open door before stepping in. Both DIs held files in their hands and were in the middle of a discussion.

Joe began first. "Sorry to interrupt—"

Irene cut him off, slapping the stolen newsprint on the desk. "We found information, gentlemen. Please say you have as well."

"We have," Lestrade said. "Do you want to go first?"

"No," Irene said. Joe's eyebrows shot up. "I need facts before speculation."

Both Inspectors eyed each other, suspicious of Irene's angle as she usually spoke out of turn.

"I have the letter Lizzie wrote to her parents," Gregory began. "Also, they didn't seem to care about her when I first spoke to them. They confirmed she'd run off with some man and seemed to not need any more information. Once I told them what had happened to their daughter, and the state we found her in, they became a bit more concerned, but not by much. They are coming to visit her—"

"Where's the letter?"

He held it up, but yanked it out of reach when Irene went to snatch it.

She made another grab for it, but he held it high. "Thom. Stop it."

As tempting as it was to let Gregory teach her a lesson, Joe knew this was not the case to do it with. Being an inch taller than the DI, Joe easily plucked the letter.

Irene's expression softened, but she still swiped it from her partner's hand. She then pointed at Joe and he got out his notebook. Annette straightened beside him, ready to listen.

"Handwriting belongs to a young woman. Quite possibly Lizzie's. Shaky due to nerves or excitement; hard to tell at this point. It's written quickly. There is a teardrop on the upper left corner. It's folded neatly, however. Meaning, she was not the one to mail it." She sniffed the envelope. "The fact that the scent of this cheap chewing tobacco remains means the kidnapper chews often and a lot. He's older, as this scent rarely appeals to younger men, and most have moved on to smoking. Lizzie wrote it under duress, and he mailed it." She handed the letter and envelope back to Gregory. "Well done, Thom. Your turn, Eddy."

Both DIs simply looked at her and, again, as much as Joe wanted to let them teach her a lesson about manners, this was not the time.

He stood beside Irene and wrapped his arm around her. "We are finding this case a bit difficult. And we are training a new assistant. So, if you could just be lenient—"

"Neither of those are true," Irene snapped. "Well, perhaps the second bit. But I am fine with this case."

Ignoring the latter statement, both DIs took Joe's words to heart and thankfully understood his plea. Lestrade clasped his partner on the shoulder and held the files out nicely for Irene. She took them gently and muttered a thank-you before flipping through them.

"There was one other case from years ago," Lestrade said. "There was no name attached to the girl. But she was lobotomised, same as Nettie, and the body was found abandoned in a house with no owner in Milford—"

"Milford? That's only a few towns over from the finishing school."

"Yes. The house has since been torn down and there was nothing odd found in any of the rooms. The lobotomy didn't kill her, though, her cause of death was starvation."

"Starvation?"

Lestrade nodded. "She was lobotomised almost a year before and left to rot in the basement of this house."

Irene went silent and leaned on the desk.

When it was clear that she wasn't going to ask any more questions, Lestrade spoke up. "Can we know what's in that paper you've brought?"

Without looking up, Irene held it out.

Lestrade and Gregory stood shoulder to shoulder to read.

Joe glanced at Annette then. She was looking at Lestrade with wide, puppy-dog-like eyes as he skimmed the article.

Joe tried to hide his smile.

"So," Lestrade said, "we don't know if he made it back to France or not."

"Exactly," Joe confirmed. "I'm not sure how it works between stations, but is there a way to phone the French police and collect his record?"

"Of course. But I don't speak one word of French."

"Oh, I do," Annette squeaked. "I speak it fluently."

"Excellent." Lestrade clapped his hands. "Come with me. We will make the call from the bigger office. Are you sure you're comfortable translating?"

"Very much so!"

Lestrade glanced at Joe, who shrugged. Annette was here to help them, and if the DI didn't have a problem with it, then neither did he. Irene was still reading the files, so everyone took that as a silent agreement.

"Jolly good. Let's go."

* * * * *

About a half hour later, Gregory entered the small office, balancing three cups in his hand. Joe took a coffee for himself and passed a tea to Irene. She spun slowly in Lestrade's chair and caught the cup on her way by. The three sipped as they waited.

When Lestrade and Annette returned, the girl's cheeks were pink with excitement; as if she'd just performed the greatest task ever for the British Government and had saved the world. She hurried over to Irene, who bumped her knee on the desk to stop her spinning.

"Well?"

"He never made it back to France," Lestrade supplied in an even tone. "They found evidence of the transport car being run off the road, so they assumed someone just 'took care' of him. Then

Germany invaded, and he wasn't a priority anymore. According to the Inspector we spoke to, he was a nasty piece of work. They didn't get a photograph of him because he didn't even make it to the station to get processed."

Irene snorted. "Scotland Yard didn't take photos when they arrested him?"

"No. Once they found out where he was from, they sent him right back."

"How did he escape?" Joe asked.

Lestrade shrugged. "They're not sure. It appeared as if he simply overpowered the transport vehicle and ran away."

Irene stood and began pacing, hands clasped behind her back. "How he escaped would be useful, but it is the *why* we are missing. *Why* did he begin these procedures again? Does he have a purpose? Or is he simply a sick man determined to mutilate women?"

"Our next stop," Lestrade said. "Is to travel out there and speak to the residents, see if anyone has seen or heard anything."

"As for the unidentified victim," Gregory chimed in, "I'll do some more digging, see if I can find out *anything* about her."

"We'll need a doctor," Lestrade said to his partner, the two in full investigator mode. "A psychologist, preferably. To testify in court to all these facts we're collecting."

The two continued to chat.

Joe glanced at Irene. She'd gone stock still and chewed the inside of her cheek, her mouth in a tight line. He subtly shuffled sideways, his elbow touching hers. This seemed to snap her out of her reverie and she stood pin straight.

"I know a doctor who will help us," she blurted, not leaving any pauses for questions. "If he is still practising, of course. I can find him tomorrow and ask him some questions."

"Oh wonderful," Gregory said. "One of us can go with you—"

"No. I will go alone."

Both DIs hesitated, shooting wary glances at each other, knowing what a disagreement could bring.

In the end, Lestrade made the sacrifice. "One of us should be there, Irene. If he is helpful—"

"Should he provide us with useful information, I shall ask him if he cares to testify, and if he will write a statement. But I will visit him alone. Now, I don't see us getting any more work done until we've spoken to this doctor, so I will bid you all a goodnight. Annette, Eddy will drive you home. You may join us again tomorrow, if you so wish. So, get a good sleep."

With that, she pivoted on her heels and walked out of the office. They all stared for a brief moment before Annette turned to Lestrade.

"I can catch the bus home. That's not a problem."

"Nonsense. Give me five minutes to file these, then I'll gladly drive you home." He caught Joe's eye and motioned for him to follow. The pair left the office to the tall filing cabinets next door.

"Try to go with Irene," Lestrade said, stuffing the files into their proper spot. "I don't believe she will fabricate anything, but we do need everything to be as accurate as possible."

"Of course. You know I will do my best."

They shook hands, and the DI glanced at Annette, who sat, prim and proper, behind his desk, waiting for him.

"Is she…" He trailed off, took a breath and started again. "I mean… It's alright that I'm giving her a ride home?"

"How do you mean?"

"I just don't want to give off the impression that I'm looking for something I am not."

"*Ah.* She is simply young and eager, but she is smart and perceptive – at least what we've seen so far. She will catch on to your intentions, especially if there are none. Unless you want there to be, of course."

"Oh, I haven't got a clue what I'm doing or what I want. I think I will worry about this mad man drilling holes in people's heads. That I do know how to solve."

Joe chuckled and clasped his hand again. "See you tomorrow."

He headed back through the trenches of Scotland Yard to wherever Irene ended up. No doubt she'd be tapping her foot, impatiently waiting for him.

Sure enough, when he exited the building, she was leaning against the Vauxhall at the side of the road. Her arms were folded across her chest as she glared at a couple of young men sauntering up the street.

"Hm," she said when Joe approach. "It took you long enough."

"It's hard to keep up with someone when they suddenly leave without warning and without saying goodbye."

She scoffed and climbed into the car, starting the engine. The ride back to Baker Street was silent, and Joe knew better than to start a conversation – mostly because traffic was quite busy and he didn't need Irene any more distracted than she was.

They arrived home and Joe took Isla out for a stroll. A plate of stew waited for him on the table when they returned and he tucked in immediately. Irene didn't join him.

As he finished his dinner, she went into the lavatory, clad in pyjamas and a robe. Joe decided to settle in for the evening as well. Once he'd washed his face and returned to the sitting area, Irene had moved into her bedroom once more. He knocked on her door and received a mumble from the other side.

He entered her room, hitting a pile of washing. "Just checking in on you."

"You keep doing that."

"I know. But this is the first case in a while where it seems to be affecting you. And I'm worried seeing this doctor tomorrow will make you even more upset and you will bottle it up inside."

She kept her gaze on the floor for a long minute, hugging her legs to her chest. Joe waited, knowing she'd eventually say something – even if it was that she didn't want to talk about it.

Irene released her knees and stretched her legs.

"This doctor was a friend of Uncle John," she finally said, staring at her toes. "He used to ask him about my father's condition. I know that when I sit down with him, he'll ask about Father and what happened with Uncle John and… I don't know if I want to. At least not with him. Only because he will tell me things that will help, but I am worried the helping might hurt."

She blew out a breath. Her words toppled over one another – a rare occurrence as she was often very articulate.

Joe sat down on the bed. The mattress bent in the middle, sending Irene gently toppling into him.

"You don't have to see him. We can find another doctor, or another way to get the information."

She was shaking her head before he even finished his sentence. "He is the best. He will help this case and we will stop this horrible man from harming more women. If my father knew I was even hesitant for one second, he would 'tsk tsk' me."

"I'm sure he wouldn't. If he knew how difficult it was for you, I don't think he would ever push you like that."

"He would encourage me, though."

Joe knew any attempt to help her further would end in an argument. Not because Irene was being difficult, but because that was her defence: she made people mad and forced them to dismiss her, thus ending the conversation. There was a fine line between pushing her gently and stepping back and letting her thoughts overwhelm her until she dismissed everyone and locked herself in her room. He was getting better at figuring out the correct way to approach his mercurial friend, and very rarely did his attempts end up with the wrong outcome.

"I know you didn't want anyone to come with you," he said, acknowledging her feelings, which was often the best way to start, "but I can. I'll wait outside in the hall, or down in the car for you. But I'll be there in case you need me."

Irene let out a soft snort. "I should be able to do it on my own."

"But you don't have to."

He saw her trying to think of a retort or excuse, but she struggled. Her worry ran deeper than simply speaking with a doctor about a case; it was something Joe had helped her work through in the past year, despite not even taking one class in psychology.

It was never easy, but she had improved.

He gently bumped her shoulder. "I know that *you* know you don't have to do anything on your own. Your own stubbornness and what you think you should be able to do gets in your way. Having someone come with you to do something that makes you uncomfortable doesn't make you a coward or any less of a person. Everyone needs back-up sometimes. Even the great Sherlock

Holmes and his equally brilliant daughter. Your father had John, and you have me."

Irene didn't say anything, but didn't move away either. They sat in silence for almost three full minutes. Joe stayed still, knowing that even her silence was progress. She hadn't snapped at him, or brushed him off, nor changed the subject. He wished she would process her thoughts out loud, but this was better than nothing.

Finally, she wrapped her arms around his bicep and pressed her cheek into his shoulder.

"I do have to learn to do it on my own, Joe. Because one day you won't be here."

Her words stung, like little pinpricks in his heart. He thought she was just uncomfortable speaking about her father with a psychologist. He hadn't even thought of him not being here to offer aid to her. His heart sped up as a panic set in.

"Where would I ever go?" His voice cracked slightly, and he hoped she wouldn't notice.

"Off with Sarah. Or another girl. Work at your vet practice. Get married. Have a life."

His lungs constricted even tighter. He wanted to say that he wasn't ever leaving Baker Street. He wouldn't even leave this room if she didn't want him to. But he knew that was false. His life had to carry on whether or not that included 221b.

Just the mere thought of leaving Baker Street right now made bile rise in his throat. He tried to breathe slowly, concentrating on

Irene's arms around his, her thumb tapping a beat on his sleeve as she processed her own thoughts. Her hair smelled like lemons and the fresh scent of wool cleaner from her hat.

His body eventually got under control. Now exhausted, and not wanting to dwell on those feeling again, he patted Irene's hand.

"Right now, my life is with you. Now tuck up."

Yawning, she released him and buried herself under her blankets. He pulled them up to her chin.

"Goodnight, Irene."

She mumbled what could have been goodnight back.

Joe turned her light off, letting his own yawn out.

Chapter VII

A Session with Doctor Roper

Doctor Roper's office was in the lower level of the university. Irene's shoes echoed as she strode down the hallway. Joe's heavy footsteps kept up, but just barely. She wasn't trying to lose him, but a part of her hoped he would simply say he would see her back at the car when she finished. But the man was determined to follow her right to the department door.

A small seating area branched off into three different offices, benches were scattered about. Irene pointed to one.

"Sit. I won't be long."

"Sit, *please*," he chided. "And take your time. Perhaps talk to him about other things while you're in there."

She rolled her eyes. "We are here to discuss the case, not me."

Joe pulled a book from his bag. "I know, but just give it some thought. At least keep an open mind about coming back here once the case is done."

"I will, if you will."

Joe's panicked episodes had practically subsided in the past year, but Irene saw small ones that he couldn't hide. Like last night while speaking in her bedroom. She hated sharing what troubled her, but she could confidently say that Joe hid his dark emotions almost better than her.

He called her bluff. "Perhaps I will."

The door to Doctor Roper's office opened. "Ah, Irene. Come on in. It was lovely to receive your call this morning."

His eyebrows were as bushy as the beard that covered his chin, and as wild as the curly hair atop his head, all salt and pepper, with bits of bright white throughout. "I wasn't sure how to get in contact with you, but I certainly tried."

The room was warm and rich, just like its occupant. While not tall, Roper stood straight and commanded attention softly. He'd filled out since Irene had seen him last, his wife keeping him well-fed since the war ended.

The older gentleman took up a seat in a chair next to a sturdy desk. Beside him was a chaise that looked quite comfortable.

"Please, have a seat."

Irene shook her head, gesturing to a smaller chair. "I'll sit there."

"Sitting in the chaise does not make this a session."

"Regardless, I shall stay here."

Doctor Roper peered at her through half rimmed glasses. "How are you? How's your father?"

Irene stiffened. She had known he'd ask, but she was still unprepared for her body's reaction.

"I'm not here to talk about him."

"Are you sure?"

"Yes. Perhaps one day I will, but not today."

The man scribbled something in the notebook in his lap.

"What did you write? This is not a session, Doctor Roper."

"I know," he said, keeping his voice even and calm. "I simply wrote the date, so I can take notes for what you need to speak to me about. Now, how can I help, Irene?"

A tiny part of her way down in her toes wanted to blurt out everything she'd been feeling since the war ended. Roper reminded her of Uncle John, and how stoic he would get when he listened to her whine about something at school or other children in the neighbourhood. He could be calmer than her father if it was to help her remain level-headed. Father had a way of getting riled up with her when she was angry about something, but Uncle John managed to keep them both from charging out the front door.

"I am working on a case," she started, choosing to stay focused on what really mattered.

"Lovely," he said, voice still steady. "I thought you might continue that after the war. How are you enjoying it?"

"Oh, uh. It's going well."

"And are you on your own?"

"In my work?"

"Work, or personal life."

"Both, I suppose. My colleague is Doctor Joe Watson and—"

"Interesting." He scribbled a note. "And a doctor at that."

"What are you writing? He is a vet, an animal doctor. And he has no relation to my uncle, obviously, and if I hadn't needed a flatmate and a place to live – and if he didn't look so sad and desperate – I wouldn't even be living at Baker Street with him, anyway."

"Oh, you are back at Baker Street?"

"I am."

"That's wonderful. Good for you."

Irene folded her arms across her chest and fixed her glare on the doctor. Her heart thudded in her ears and the urge to tell him how wonderful she was doing almost overwhelmed her. She wanted to blurt out how, despite pushing her father out of her head every chance she got throughout the war, she was now considering writing him a letter. And that, despite swearing to never return to Baker Street after Uncle John's death, she now hosted Christmas and even displayed photographs of her father and uncle.

Instead, she picked a fluff off her trousers. "I would like to discuss the case I am working on."

A soft smile came across Roper's wrinkled face. "We certainly can. You did well containing what looked to be quite an outburst."

Her jaw tightened and her heart had yet to slow down, but again, Irene maintained her composure. "Thank you."

Joe would be proud if he saw her. She knew it was out of pure stubbornness that she remained as calm as she did. If she snapped, said something dismissive, or got up and walked away, Doctor Roper would win.

Or perhaps the man genuinely cared about her.

Regardless, she cleared her throat and started into the facts.

"Two women were found – escaped rather – from a man performing lobotomies on them. Two different procedures that left them both relatively mute, with slower reflexes than a turtle."

He frowned. "One with holes in her temple and the other with two black eyes, correct?"

"That's right."

"There is an American doctor who changed the original procedure from drilling holes to sticking ice picks through the eye sockets. It's not as invasive, nor does it take as long. It's a very recent discovery. So, your culprit is keeping up his medical knowledge."

"That sounds horrifically painful. Which means wherever he is doing the procedures is away from any prying neighbours."

"It's a harsh procedure," the doctor nodded, "and I don't believe it works at all. The brain is complicated; poking at it with a stick when we don't have a full understanding of it doesn't do anyone any good."

"Then why do it at all?" Irene asked, more to herself than Roper, but he answered anyway.

"To subdue. To cure hysterical or radical behaviour. If he is keeping up with the studies, then it sounds like he is actively trying to cure someone."

"Or he is deluded."

"How do you figure?"

"He was arrested for performing these operations illegally before the war, then he escaped capture. So, perhaps he thinks his original patient is still alive."

"Perhaps she is, and he has yet to perform the procedure on her."

Irene stood and paced. "We have a report of an unnamed victim, with holes in her head, that was found close to where these two women escaped from. She died from starvation, as if she was just left in the house. Perhaps he doesn't even know she is dead. At least, that's my hope."

"I can't imagine he'd continue on knowing she was dead."

Irene couldn't help but smirk as she saw a way to best the doctor. "People are capable of all sorts of atrocities. We had a case last year where a father kept the corpse of his daughter in the attic and would bring her food."

Doctor Roper sucked in a breath. "That... That's truly horrendous, Irene. Do you solve cases that dark often?"

She shook her head. "Not often. Usually there is more action. More guns."

He made a note.

"These women you found," he pivoted. "Were they bound?"

"Yes." Irene continued pacing, glad he kept the conversation to the case.

"And was anything else done to them?"

"No," she said, catching his meaning. "Just the procedure."

"Then he is doing this for the sole purpose of the lobotomy and what he hopes to gain from practise. In any case, you must work fast. Such men don't like their work interrupted. He will be on the hunt for another young woman."

"Precisely," Irene stopped pacing. "When we capture him, will you testify in court to how dangerous these procedures are? You may have to meet his victims."

"I will certainly do that."

"Thank you, Doctor. Truly."

Roper stood and extended a hand. "Please ring, should you have any other questions."

"Of course. What notes did you write about me?"

He chuckled. "Come back when this case is complete and we shall talk about everything."

"I don't want to talk about everything. I want to know what you wrote about me."

"Only promising things. It was absolutely lovely to see you."

He walked her to the door.

Joe stood as he saw them.

"Ah, Joe Watson, I presume," Roper said.

"I am. Please to meet you."

They clasped hands, and the Doctor nodded toward Irene. "When this case is finished, you bring her back to me."

Irene huffed. "I don't need to come back here. Talk to Joe, instead. He's been through more hell than me."

"Doctor Watson is more than welcome to visit me also."

"Perhaps we both will," Joe said.

Irene scoffed. "Come, Joe. We have a madman to find. Goodbye Doctor Roper, and thank you."

"Take care, Irene."

She had no intention of coming back here. At least, that was her first thought. But as she recalled how easily he'd extracted information from her, and how – very oddly – speaking about certain things with a professional who understood her brain more than most, might just be helpful.

Of course, she had her partner and flatmate, who knew her better than even a psychologist. But poor Joe had his own troubles.

She scowled again as she neared the end of the hall. All that took work and focus, and right now she needed to turn that energy to finding their culprit.

* * * * *

Eddy and Annette were waiting at Baker Street when the pair returned. They all munched on chips Miss Hudson had made, discussing the next step of the case. It was obvious that a trip out to Milford was needed. It was a two-hour drive, but one they could easily make by the late afternoon.

"We don't all need to travel out there," Eddy said, eyeing Annette. "I can take a couple of constables and—"

"And do what?" Irene interrupted him with a mouth full of food. "Sit around and hope he pops up in a pub? No, that won't do."

"This man is—"

"Dangerous, I know. We've faced worse, though. We have to find where he is taking these women. What would be even better is if we could draw him out. Perhaps that is the solution while we look for his operating room."

Irene felt everyone's eyes on her, but that didn't matter. She was on the verge of an idea; she just needed the gears to catch up to her thoughts.

The same nervous high returned, like at Doctor Roper's. She was excited and ready to solve this case. And she felt vulnerable.

She needed a win.

Annette hung on her every word, her big eyes waiting for the solution.

Perhaps she *was* the solution.

"Draw him out?" Eddy spoke first. "How? Offer up free medical supplies and a paper on the new lobotomy technique?"

"That would be ridiculous."

"Well, of course it's ridiculous. I was—"

"We use bait."

Both Eddy and Joe sighed in unison. The young girl, however, appeared as if she had stars in her eyes.

Joe shook his head. "I really don't like it when you put yourself in harm's way."

Irene waved him off. "He won't go for me."

"Why not?"

"I'm too old."

She kept staring at Annette, willing her to speak. She could offer her up, of course, but even to Irene, that seemed crass. So, she bore her eyes into her assistant's, hoping she'd come to the realization on her own.

"I can do it," Annette said finally. "I can be the bait."

"No." Both men spoke together.

"It's our only choice," Irene argued.

"It's really not," Eddy stood to debate, towering over her.

"It is. Annette is the exact type of woman this man goes after. That dead body was a petite woman with a blonde bob, exactly like her. We'd be fools not to use her."

"Annette is not a tool to be used," Joe snapped.

"Of course not. She is my assistant—"

"*Our* assistant. And I'm not letting her do this."

Isla crawled out from under the couch and huffed at the noise.

"Then what else do we do? Walk around whistling for him? Visit every bloody house in the countryside looking for an operating room?"

"If it keeps her out of harm's way—"

"Annette, do you want to help us?"

Joe scoffed. "When you put the question like that, she is going to say yes."

Isla started barking, low and steady.

"We need to stop him. And for that to happen—"

Joe stepped even closer. "You do this time and time again. No more bait. No more asking other people to be bait."

"What else shall we do? Eddy's plan? Attempt to lure him out with a fat carrot? *She* will be the carrot."

"Listen to yourself, Irene."

Isla raised her barks to high-pitched yips.

"Isla, please!" Irene snapped.

Annette jumped up. "I'll take her out."

Eddy cleared his throat. "I shall step out with you and let the air diffuse in here." He stepped between the pair. "And do let it diffuse. We will figure out a solution. You two fighting really throws me off."

Eddy followed Annette out. Once they were gone, Irene pivoted on her heel.

"Where are you going?" Joe snapped.

"To the loo," she snapped back.

She stood inside the small room with her fists clenched. They had to use Annette. There was no other way.

Why had Joe gotten so mad? He seemed fine this morning.

Sure, she'd used herself as bait before, but she always made it out alive. And they always solved the case.

Irene splashed some cold water on her face, then dried it using a towel that Miss Hudson kept insisting was a guest towel.

She opened the door and ran right into Joe.

"What are—"

He crowded her back into the lavatory, shutting the door.

"I know you want to catch him, but you cannot let him take her."

"It's the best bet to get him. If he wanted older women, then I would gladly step in and let him take me."

"I certainly would let *that* happen, either."

Irene folded her arms across her chest. She understood Joe's point – it wasn't ideal to have Annette as bait. But there was no other choice.

"Perhaps I can switch off with Annette. Get his attention with her, then offer myself—"

"No."

"Joe—"

"No, Irene." His voice was deep and firm. "It's not worth it. We've got plenty of information from criminals by observing and questioning them."

"And what if we can't find him again? What if he runs, or overpowers us, or… I don't know. This is the plan. If you do not want to follow along, then you can stay home."

"You know I won't do that."

"Then accept it."

A sharp knock came at the door. Before either of them could react, Eddy slipped inside the tiny room with them.

"What are you two doing in here?"

Joe sighed and turned to him, almost coming nose to nose, before pausing and turning back to Irene. "We're discussing—"

"Nothing, we're finished."

From out in the sitting room, Miss Hudson's voice greeted Annette. "Hello dear, where is everyone?"

"I think in the lavatory."

Irene gave Joe a shove, who bumped into Eddy. "Out, both of you."

The door behind them opened and hit Eddy's shoulder.

Miss Hudson was right outside, hands on her hips. "I don't know what you three are doing in there, and I don't want to know. Now, come and get your tea."

Eddy squeezed out first.

Before Joe left, he paused and glanced at Irene. "Please think about this plan."

"I think about everything."

He sighed and left her alone in the lavatory.

* * * * *

Irene and Joe were in the Vauxhall, while Eddy and Annette followed in his Wolseley. The drive took all afternoon; it was almost teatime when they arrived in Milford.

Irene stretched as soon as she was out of the car. Joe groaned as he did the same, reaching his long arms to the sky.

They entered the pub where Lizzie and Nettie were taken months ago – the same place where Irene and Joe had questioned the barkeep during that case. Luckily, it was him behind the counter today.

Eddy and Annette stepped in behind them. As per their plan, the young woman sat alone at a corner table, pulling out a book.

Irene glanced around at the other patrons. Half a dozen sat at tables, drinking and eating, but the pub wasn't nearly as full as it would be in a few hours once everyone was off work.

Not one man fit the description of their culprit, either.

Doubt stirred in her stomach as she made her way to the bartender. What if this was a bad idea? What if this man never showed up? What if he already skipped town?

She shook her head. This was the current plan, and they needed to focus on it, or else this trip *would* be wasted.

"Hey, I remember you two," the barkeep came up to her. "Looking for a girl, right?"

"Correct."

"You ever find her?"

"One of them, yes," she said, producing the pictures of Nettie and Lizzie. "These two women were both in here in the past few months chatting with the same man."

"Yeah, that's right. They were real friendly. Then left with him."

"Would you recognize that man if he walked into this pub?"

"'Course. He was in here not two days ago. Ate come chips. Comes in around supper, usually for a bit of fish. Not sure where he lives, but he looked unwell, let me tell you."

"Excellent. Thank you."

Irene pointed to a table in the opposite corner of Annette, where she and Joe sat down and waited.

Almost two hours and three baskets of chips later, Irene rubbed her eyes and yawned. "Say something interesting to me, Joe."

He stuttered, as if he'd just woken up from a nap. "To date, there are four different species of giraffes."

"That's not interesting."

"I think it is. Who knew that many giraffes existed?" He sipped at his tea, which he kept refilling, and then travelling to the lavatory. "I will admit, I am getting nervous and I have been snappy at you."

"You have."

"But *you* have to admit that this is a very dangerous case and my worry is not without warrant."

"It is not."

"Then, why don't we leave—"

"No," Irene said. "We're too close to catching him. If he doesn't show up tonight, then we will scour the town. But he was here two days ago. He will show up again."

"I worry people will get hurt."

"I don't care if I get hurt."

"I do, though," he hissed. "I worry about you."

The pub door dinged and a tall, slim, and very frazzled-looking man entered. The bartender greeted him, then looked at Irene and Joe.

At the same time, the man spotted Annette.

"Put that worry aside, Joe," Irene said. "This is our man."

Chapter VIII
Chasing a Madman Down the Street

The man immediately put Joe on edge. Though he didn't exactly look evil, there was an unsettling air about him. His clothes were a bit too askew, and his hair was a tad too long. Beneath it all, and with some effort, he was probably once handsome, which is how he attracted his victims.

He sat across from Annette, and she giggled politely at his greeting. In unison, Joe, Irene and Eddy all stood. It was dramatic and the wrong move all at once.

The man noticed the shadows against the wall.

Lestrade put out his hand to calm him before he could even speak. "Please come with me quietly."

Beside Joe, Irene backed toward the door, blocking the exit.

When their culprit didn't move, Lestrade grasped his shoulder. Like a switch, the man lept into action. He grabbed a beer glass and flung it at Lestrade. The DI ducked, and the glass hit the bar. The man tipped the table toward Annette, causing Lestrade to reach for her. With the DI out of the way, the man took off toward the door.

Joe attempted to stop him, but he turned and swung another beer glass. Two men sitting near the door intervened, but got shoved aside harshly. The man chucked yet another glass, this time at Irene. She ducked, cussing, as he sailed past her and out into the evening. She immediately shot after him.

"Irene, wait!" Joe called, running out as well.

The man was several metres ahead, struggling to run. He suddenly pulled a gun from his waistband; the barrel glinting in the setting sun.

Joe tackled Irene to the ground behind the Vauxhall. A bullet whirred over their heads, hammering the brick of the pub.

Irene popped to her feet, firing two shots back at him.

Joe had no idea where her gun came from, but he grabbed for her again. She shook him off as the man fired back. The bullet stuck in the pavement a metre away from Joe. A phantom pain coursed through his side where he was shot a few months ago and he cried out, clutching his stomach.

The roar of an automobile engine caught his attention, and he flattened himself to the ground, peering under the Vauxhall. A dark blue car sped away up the road.

Irene fired again, the sound piercing his ears.

Brakes squealed from around the corner and metal crunched.

"Aha!" she cried and hurried around their car.

"No!" Joe reached for her, but she was gone.

He dragged himself up and hurried after her. Every instinct told him to run *away* from the madman with the gun, but there was no way he was letting Irene dive head-first.

His side ached and his chest was tight, sweat beading on his forehead as he scrambled to catch up to his partner.

"Wait, Irene. Please."

The man's car was turned, blocking most of the road. The tire was flat and the driver's door was splayed open.

Irene cussed and stared down the empty road.

People stepped out onto the main road to view the ruckus, but the man was long gone.

A woman yelled, "He took my car!"

"Make and colour," Irene snapped.

"It's red."

Irene crouched by the tires of the abandoned auto. "Joe, look. Pine needles, dirt and…" She pried a leaf from the tread of the flattened tire. "Do you remember that street with the willow trees? You remarked on how they are your favourite tree and I said they might be mine too?"

Joe's chest still ached. He rubbed his heart. It took him a moment as he was still trying to process the foot chase. "Vaguely."

"That's where he's driven down. I know where he is."

"What about my car?" the lady cried.

"We will get your car back. Now please go away. You're distracting."

Lestrade and Annette finally caught up to them.

"How did this go so wrong?" the DI snapped.

Irene didn't answer, just continued poking at the culprit's car.

Joe shook his head, his breath finally coming back to him. "We didn't expect him to have a gun."

"But we should've," Irene said, still grasping the willow leaf. "He is clearly violent. We should've expected it."

"There's no point chasing him now," Lestrade said. "Especially if you know where he's headed. We know what he looks like, and we know what he escaped in. I will call some constables and we will scour the entire countryside—"

Irene headed back toward the Vauxhall without listening.

Lestrade threw his hands in the air.

"Let me talk to her," Joe said. "She's just angry right now."

Lestrade nodded, hands on his hips, glancing at Annette. She stood statue still, unsure of what to do.

Joe's heart still thrummed in his ears as he approached their car. He had been practically incapacitated because of the state the gunshots had put him in. With his senses coming back to him, anger seeped through the dissipating panic. That whole affair had been chaotic and dangerous. Irene had put herself at serious risk. By the time he got to the Vauxhall, he was fuming, heart in his ears all over again.

Irene was in the driver's seat already, the engine on.

He flung the passenger door open. "We're not chasing him, Irene. He's got a gun. Let Ed and the other constables take care of him."

"Eddy doesn't have a gun."

"Give him yours."

"I'm not handing over my uncle's gun."

"Dammit." Joe smacked the car hard enough to make it rock. "Why are you like this sometimes?"

"Why are you so protective sometimes and other times not?"

"I don't know. But for once, I'd like you to just let someone else handle it."

"Maybe next time. Are you coming or not?"

She stared out the front window even though she was well aware that Joe wouldn't let her drive away without him.

He climbed in the car and slammed the door shut. He'd deal with this whole issue once they were safely back at Baker Street. Right now, he had to make sure this woman wasn't driving off to her death.

There was nothing for him to hang on to as she sped off down the road. Right toward the car blocking the street.

"How are you going to—"

Irene jerked the steering wheel. The car bounced over the curb, two wheels on the road, the other two on the pavement.

He held on to the dashboard, bracing himself against her turns. She finally returned the car to the road, the axle making an awful squeaking sound. Joe sat back, hands shaking uncontrollably, and he tried to take deep breaths to keep this panic at bay. It fought back, though, squeezing his lungs and pressing on his stomach.

Irene glanced at him. "Are you injured?"

"What?" he said, still breathless. "No."

"Then why are your hands shaking?"

"Because that was terrifying." His voice cracked, and he didn't try to hide it.

"I am in complete control of this vehicle, Joe. So don't—"

"It's not the vehicle, it was being shot at. It was making sure you *weren't* being shot at. This whole damn thing."

"But you've been shot at before."

"The last time it happened, I was hit." He winced again as the imaginary pain snaked through his stomach.

"But you've been in danger since."

Fury bubbled inside of him. He rarely got angry at Irene. Frustrated and exasperated? At least once a week. But his anger spilled over now,

"I don't know why this happened, okay? Maybe your doctor friend can figure it out."

She went silent. Her fingers gripped the steering wheel, knuckles white, as they drove out of town.

His fury turned to guilt, flipping in his stomach like a heavy flapjack. He was angry, yes, but the quip about the doctor was unnecessary. Of course, she'd made worse comments to him about various subject matters, but his words came out so viciously.

As he opened his mouth to apologize, Irene pointed out the front window. "There's his car."

The abandoned automobile was parked next to a forest that led into a shallow ravine. Irene pulled up behind it, and Joe hurried out behind her. The driver's door was wide open, one tire was punctured.

"Do we follow him or find the house?"

Irene started into the ravine. "The house. He will eventually return to it, and if not, Eddy can get some dogs out here to track him. But I need to find out where he kept these women."

Joe glanced back down into the ravine, almost preferring to go after the man, as he knew the crime scene they were about to find would be absolutely horrible.

* * * * *

Just as the sun dipped beyond the horizon, Irene slowed in front of a rather derelict building. It was set back from the road, through a brick wall with a small metal gate. The darkness turned the area into a horror novel. Dead trees twisted their way to the sky and dry brambles curled over the gate that hung from broken hinges.

Irene stooped at the front walk, poking at some leaves, before standing and heading to the gate. She examined the hinges as Joe came up beside her.

"He hasn't arrived yet. At least not through here. We will forgo the front door and search for a cellar around back."

He didn't argue. He really didn't want to walk through the front door of a house that looked ready to sprout teeth and swallow them up.

Every window looked covered in heavy curtains, and Joe saw no movement from within. They quickly picked their way through the overgrown garden to the rear of the house. A cellar door stuck up from the ground, the surrounding grass trampled and flattened.

There was no lock on the door, which was curious. As Irene crouched to study it, Joe searched in the grass. He found a lock, ripped from the wood, in a tall pile of weeds.

"They knocked it clean off."

"It didn't take much." Irene pointed to the shallow divots in the door. "Decaying wood and rusty metal. All it would've taken is one solid push."

"Then why not escape sooner?"

"Either the sound of him locking the door deterred them, or he had them secured with chains or rope inside the cellar, then discarded it after the procedure." She wrenched a door open. "We shall go down and see."

She let the door down gently and dropped her bag. Joe fished a torch from his own bag and clicked it on. He followed Irene down the stepladder and immediately gagged. The floor was hard under his feet and the room smelled horrible. Blood, urine, and metal, mixed with decaying wood and dry, packed dirt filled the space. He lit up the far corner. A single mattress was shoved against the wall in between a few buckets.

Metal clanging against itself sounded from the opposite corner. Joe swung his light toward it. Irene reached up to a chain and pulled. Bright white light flooded the room, illuminating a hospital table and chair. A cart sat next to the table, full of medical equipment; a bottle of a powerful sleeping barbiturate sat half empty next to used needles.

"No wonder Nettie lost her mind in the hospital."

Irene plucked an ice pick from the pile, the tip stained dark with blood or some other fluid.

"This is monstrous," she whispered.

Joe watched her for a moment. Usually, she attacked crime scenes with intense vigour and an almost gleeful demeanour. Now, however, her brow was furrowed, her shoulders drooped, and she lingered with her jaw clenched, simply looking at everything.

"Irene?" Joe spoke softly, trying to get her attention.

She picked up a small mallet and studied it.

"Those girls must've been so scared."

She glanced at the corner where the mattress was, then flung the mallet against the wall.

"Lizzie was here because of us."

"What do you mean?"

She snorted in disgust. "She went missing, and we gave up looking for her."

Joe had that same thought at the hospital, and it still sat like a stone in his gut. Irene wasn't wrong, but…

"All the evidence pointed to her running away with a man," he said, trying to comfort both of them. "Between the interview with her parents, the school, and the fact that her family received a letter from her, it made sense that she ran away."

"We should've found that letter and studied it. I would've known right away something was wrong. That entire case was askew. I was not myself. I could've done better."

He stepped closer to her, wishing they could have this conversation somewhere other than a horrid crime scene. "Both girls are safe now. We can't go back in time, unfortunately. What we can do is keep investigating and capture this guy so he can't do this to any more women."

"Oh, you're right. I just…" She glanced over at the mattress again.

He blocked her view and took hold of her arms. "Let's go see the rest of the house."

Irene stared directly into his eyes. It unnerved him; he wasn't quite sure what to do, so he stared back and let her work out whatever she needed to.

He let his hands drop to hers, intertwining their fingers.

"You're correct," she said, squeezing his hands. "And I apologize for making you squirm. I just needed to stare at something that wasn't this crime scene for a moment."

He squeezed her fingers back. "Never a problem. I'm glad my eyeballs provided comfort."

This drew a smile from her. Looking back at the room, she said, "It worries me that he has not returned yet, but regardless. We will explore the rest of the house."

Joe followed her to the stairs and into the back garden.

The front door opened easy enough and they both cautiously stepped inside, shining their torches around. The house wasn't much nicer than the cellar. Each room smelled mustier than the last. The rooms were barren, except for a bed and dresser in the first-floor sitting room. An office was situated at the back of the house with a chair and desk full of letters and notebooks. The walls bore a girl's name: *Janet*. The letters were frantic, some descending into scrawls.

Irene searched through a pile of papers while Joe eyed a small stack of photographs. Most of the photos were of medical procedures. One caught his eye: a young woman, with the name Janet Larrs written beneath.

The unnamed victim from the police file.

Beside Joe, Irene held out a piece of paper. "Janet Larrs went into a mental hospital. She was discharged by her brother, Gordon, a year later. There is an address – the same house where the body was found."

Joe skimmed the report. Janet hadn't been operated on in the hospital, which meant…

"He operated on his own sister? Then what? It didn't work, so he kept going? It was clear he kept visiting her after the operation, then he simply stopped. Why?"

"The war," Irene said, still poking through the papers. "There were Americans and Canadians crawling all over the hills, training. I bet he wouldn't have risked visiting her with that many people. A soldier probably found her. Then the house was torn down. He may have been in such a delusion that he didn't even realise how much time had passed."

"But the war has been over for two years. How has he not been back to that site?"

"Perhaps he forgot where it was? This is a man not right in the head."

The metal gate in the front garden clanged shut. Irene and Joe dropped to the ground, shutting off the torches. Irene crawled slowly to the window and peered out. She looked back at Joe who could just make out her nod from the dim moonlight.

Gordon Larrs was home.

They both looked toward the front door, expecting it to open. Instead, the cellar door banged. They both hurried out of the house. Sure enough, the cellar was wide open. Irene slammed it shut and Gordon Larrs' muffled cry came from inside.

"Excellent," Joe said. "Let me find something to barricade him."

Before Joe could move, the door flung open, Gordon ready to confront Irene. Joe lurched forward to grab her out of harm's way. She jerked out of his grasp and kicked Gordon square in the chest. The large man crashed backward into the cellar.

Irene followed him into the dark.

Cursing, Joe went through the door. He stumbled, almost tripping on the ladder and crashing into Irene. She waited at the bottom as Gordon struggled to his feet. As soon as he got a foot under him, she kicked him hard in the back. He flew forward, crashing into a wooden pole. Even though he was surprised, if he gained his footing, he'd be a decent match for Irene.

Joe skirted around them to the medical cart and swiped the bottle of barbital. He grabbed a syringe off the second shelf and drew a dose.

Thankfully, Gordon was still down. Joe dropped to his knees and leaned on the man's arm. The needle went in easily, the drug entering his system. After emptying the syringe, Joe jumped back, his veterinary training telling him that his patient might bite him – and in this case, he just might.

Gordon thrashed around for half a second, but the medication took effect quickly. He stayed on his hands and knees, swaying a bit before slumping to the floor.

"No!" Irene cried. "You've knocked him out!"

"Yes, I have." Joe grabbed her arm, rougher than he meant to, but he needed to get her out of here before the man woke up or she took her anger out on him.

"We need to question him!"

"We can do that at Scotland Yard."

Joe only released her when they made it to the stairs, blocking her from moving back into the room. She danced around, attempting to slip past him, but there was no room.

"Irene, no." He snapped at her, as if taking charge of a large animal, his vet training still in full effect.

She paused and glanced up at him, her jaw set, as if she had a thousand arguments on the tip of her tongue. But she thought better and pursed her lips.

"Fine." She pivoted and marched up the stairs and into the back garden.

Chapter IX

Scotland Yard Finishes the Case

They waited less than ten minutes before Eddy pulled up in his Wolseley. Joe leaned against the house, clearly exhausted.

Irene couldn't stop pacing. She kept thinking of the information she could've extracted from Gordon Larrs before Joe knocked him out. It was the right decision, but she still didn't like it. She needed answers and a conclusion to this case, and she wanted it before they all made the journey back to Scotland Yard.

Eddy's vehicle crunched on the gravel and dry grass. He cut the engine and climbed out of the car, slamming the door. He immediately stormed towards Irene. Before he could speak, she pointed to the cellar.

"Our culprit is in there, heavily sedated. There are no other women, and we found out the identity of the unnamed victim."

Eddy threw his hands in the air. "Great. You've solved it then. Would've liked to have been there to keep this as official as possible."

"Well, I—"

He cut her off, closing in on her. "Next time, tell me where you're going, for *god's sake*. You hear me?"

"I did tell you."

"'A street with willow trees' doesn't help me much."

She'd rarely seen Eddy this angry, and it made her shrink back a bit. "Fine."

The DI shook his head. "You and Joe get back to Baker Street. And *stay there*. First thing tomorrow, you will be at Scotland Yard, in my office, ready to give your statement."

"Collect the photos and letters from inside the house—"

"I know how to conduct a search. Go home."

Two other police vehicles pulled up and a handful of constables exited.

Irene peered through them. "Where's Annette?"

"I sent her home with a constable because she didn't need any more involvement, either. She will give her own statement tomorrow as well."

Joe came up to them, and Eddy shot him a glare. He averted his gaze from the DI and walked away. "I'll be in the car."

"Fine, we will go home," Irene said. "We will stop at the hospital and tell them the good news—"

"No. *I* will stop at the hospital because it is *my* job."

She scowled and folded her arms. Her friend stared at her, but neither one of them was budging.

"I get it." Eddy finally softened, placing his hands on her shoulders. "I am forever grateful for your help, you know that. But you need to learn to listen to me. The rules are changing. How we do things in court are changing. I can't have some criminal wandering free because something went wrong with their arrest because you interfered. Private investigation cases are very different from murder and criminal activity. Do you understand?"

There was no argument she could make to him. He was correct in every sense. It didn't make her feel any better; she thought of a million things she could have done differently with this case, as with every case she worked. But she didn't want to argue.

"I understand."

"Excellent." He gave her shoulders a squeeze. "Fill up on petrol before you leave town. It's a long, dark drive before another station."

Irene glanced at the cellar once more before heading to the Vauxhall. Hopefully Larrs would stay asleep all night and she'd be able to make it to Scotland Yard before they interviewed him.

To her surprise, Joe was in the driver's seat as she approached. She climbed in the passenger side.

"Why are you driving?" She asked, as he started down the laneway.

"Because you've had an emotional day. And you aren't particularly fond of driving in the dark."

She scrunched her nose. "How do you know that?"

"You're tense whenever it's after sunset and we've gone anywhere. And you offer me the keys way more often in the evening if ever we go out together."

It was true. Driving in the dark wasn't her favourite, no matter how much she liked to be in control.

She leaned her head against the cool glass as the day finally caught up to her. She felt like there was still so much left to do with this case. There'd been no interrogation. No good news delivered. All the pieces of the puzzle were in, but she hadn't stepped back to take a last look. It was all Eddy's job now. She'd have to come to terms with that, just as if there were any cases like this in the future. It was still difficult, though, no matter how much sense it made.

* * * * *

Their drive home was mostly silent until about halfway through, when Joe spoke. "I'm sorry for getting cross with you back home. And at the pub. I just worry."

"I know you worry. But this is our job."

He sighed. "And I want it to keep being our job. I know you can handle yourself. I just feel like I'm not doing my job as your partner, or friend, if I am not pointing out the risks."

She picked at her fingernail, exhausted, and ready for a cup of tea. "Keep pointing them out. Because I do get too eager and fail to see them for myself. And then I attack madmen who've been giving lobotomies without a second thought."

"Horrendously foolish, by the way."

"You subdued him, though." A smile tugged at her lips.

"My best mate was about to go toe-to-toe with him. What else was I to do? I certainly didn't want to get injured myself."

"Ah, wouldn't want to mess up that pretty face of yours." A full smile stretched across her face.

"It's the only thing I have going for me."

She couldn't see Joe in the dark of the night, but she could hear the grin in his voice.

"That's not true, and you know it. It's the second. The best thing you have going for you is that you know me."

"Friends in high places."

"Precisely."

They both chuckled, tired and ready for bed.

* * * * *

Despite the activities the night before, the following morning found Irene awake early. She hoped to get to Scotland Yard as Gordon Larrs awoke.

Joe hadn't made it downstairs yet, and she hadn't heard him stir. She hadn't even roused Miss Hudson for any sort of breakfast, as that would waste time that she did not have.

As she grabbed her hat, the telephone rang. She thought about letting it ring, but answered it, anyway. "Baker Street."

"You can take your shoes and hat off." Eddy's voice sounded tired but pleased for such an early morning.

"Oh?"

"Larrs woke late last night. Apparently, the drugs in his system were so old that they didn't have as much of a lasting effect. Once he found where he was, he confessed."

"Ah, damn." Irene tugged her hat off. "I wanted to be there. I don't suppose you told him to shut up and tell the story this morning?"

"No. They rang me at home. I interviewed him overnight. He confessed to taking Lizzie and Nettie, and three others, who are buried on the property. He denies that his sister is dead, but admitted to performing a lobotomy on her. We've contacted the French police, but will process his crimes here, as he fled during the war, and we can count his crimes in England."

Irene sighed. All of this was good news, of course. Larrs in jail for the rest of his life. Two girls safe with their families. But she wanted to see this case through, despite Eddy telling her that this was most definitely a police matter.

"You are more than welcome to read the files. I can at least do that since you were quite the help, no matter how angry I got."

"Thank you, I suppose."

"Now, I am going to finish this paperwork and go back home to bed. Cheers, Irene. And good work."

She hung up and stared at the telephone, arms drooping at her side, her plan for the day ruined. There had to be *something* she could do to wrap this case up in her mind.

The door behind her opened and Joe stumbled into the room, still half asleep.

"What's going on? You're not going to Scotland Yard, are you?"

"Of course not. The man already confessed. I'm going to the hospital to say a final goodbye to Lizzie and Nettie."

"Okay," he shuffled past her. "Do you want me to come?"

She stuck her hat back on. "No need. I shall see you later. Oh, I haven't fed Isla yet." She glanced at the dog, splayed out on her back in her bed near Joe's desk, fast asleep.

* * * * *

Irene didn't know what she would find at the hospital or if she was even allowed to visit Nettie or Lizzie. Regardless, she marched down the hallway. Nettie's parents stepped out at the same moment she arrived.

The girl's mother saw her and clasped her hands together. "Oh, we were just speaking about you, Miss Holmes."

"Is everything okay?" She peered into the room. Nettie and Lizzie both sat on the bed, notepads in each of their hands.

"Everything is as good as it could be," Mrs. Lawson said. "We've decided to take Lizzie into our home. We met her parents last night and they seem like such a nightmare. So, she is coming to live with us. She and Nettie can heal together."

Irene wanted to ask a dozen more questions regarding their other daughter, Marg, and if she'd confessed to seeing Nettie being taken. She also wanted to know how they planned to have Nettie and Lizzie heal.

"That's quite nice of you," she said instead.

Tears welled in Mrs. Lawson's eyes. "It's the least we could do. This way, they each have a friend who knows what the other's been through and they can encourage one another."

"Quite right."

"Also, DI Lestrade rang us last night to say you captured the horrid man that did this and that there is no chance of him being released from jail."

"That is correct."

The woman let out a squeal, tears in her eyes, wrapping Irene in a tight hug. "Thank you ever so much. We don't know how to repay you. We truly don't."

"It's just the job," she said, fists clenched.

The husband must've noticed, because he gently pried his wife off of Irene. "I deal with high-end furnishings. Mostly office equipment; desks, shelving, bookcases. Should you ever need to redecorate, please let us know." He dug a business card from his wallet and handed it to her.

Irene slipped it into her bag.

"Thank you. I must go. Please do not hesitate to send an update on Nettie and Lizzie's progress." She glanced once more into the hospital room. Both women looked at the paper and then at each other. After a few seconds, they both burst out into odd laughter.

Irene headed out of the hospital. While she had sympathy for the victims in their cases, those two women held the top spot. She couldn't imagine her brain taken away from her. Perhaps it was good that this case had ended, as parts of it were quite difficult to digest.

She sat in the Vauxhall but didn't know where to go.

Well, there was one place she could visit. She didn't really want to, but that was the only part left to give her some closure.

Or open up a whole new can of worms.

* * * * *

Irene pivoted on her heel in the empty hallway of the university and marched a few steps before turning back toward the small collection of offices. She hesitated in the foyer.

She finally took a deep breath and rapped on the door.

The doctor was quick to answer and a pleasant smile befell his face when he saw her. "Ah, Irene. Lovely to see you again."

She kept her demeanour as professional as possible. "I only need five minutes, if that's alright."

Doctor Roper stepped back, inviting her in. "Of course. I don't have an appointment for another hour. Have a seat."

She eyed the chaise lounge, remembering the chair she sat in last time wasn't nearly as comfortable as that couch appeared. She sat forward at the edge, with her back straight, hopefully making it clear that she wasn't here for a session, but rather a quick conversation.

The Doctor took up a seat in the chair he occupied last time they spoke. He had his notebook ready again, but said nothing.

And neither did Irene.

He looked at her with a friendly, soft expression, as if he had all the time in the world to spend with her.

She chewed her lip, knowing what she wanted to ask him, but unsure of how to start the conversation. Perhaps, like she usually did, she should just jump in with both feet.

"There is no cure for a fading mind, is there?" She stared at the floor, not wanting to see the judgement on Doctor Roper's face for how little she knew of her father's disease.

"I'm afraid not. There are ways to prolong the fading memory, but not stop it completely."

She nodded, the urge to leave almost taking her feet to the door. She got her answer, there was no reason to make the small lump in her throat grow any larger. But another part of her was so bloody curious and wanted to know everything, no matter how painful.

"Is there a way to assess the level at which the brain has diminished?"

"There is to an extent, but that is usually told by friends or family members that knew the person."

She nodded, but kept her gaze on the dark office carpet.

"Are we speaking about your father?"

"We are." Irene finally looked up at him but was only met with the same friendly face. No judgement. No pity. Simply a listening ear.

He nodded at her. "John came to me just before the war started. He saw Sherlock's condition diminishing and asked me all sorts of questions."

Her gaze dropped back to the floor, a new lump hooking on to the previous, this one spiked and painful. "Yes, well, that information was lost when he went."

"I am sorry to hear that, by the way," he said, and the first hint of emotion entered the Doctor's voice. Not pity, but genuine sadness. "The war claimed a lot of lives and it's truly not fair."

Her stomach flip-flopped. The urge to spit out all the anger bubbled up like some sort of sick and almost overtook her. Her lip curled in anger and she blew sharply out of her nose.

Sitting straight, she looked at Roper. "Perhaps one day we will talk about Uncle John and how I played a part in his death—"

Irene clamped her mouth shut. She'd never admitted that out loud before, certainly not to someone she'd barely spoken to. If she believed in magic, she would assume this room had some sort of curse on it to trick people into spilling their secrets.

The man scribbled something in his notebook. "I would love to help you work through those feelings—"

"Right now," she bit out, "I want to know if you'll assess my father. Go out to his farm with Miss Hudson, who I'm sure you remember. You knew Father before his decline, so you can assess him fairly, and give me any tips on how to help him. I will pay you your hourly wage, or whatever fee you want."

She shoved her hands under her thighs to keep them from shaking but looked at him, as if challenging him to say no.

Roper closed his notebook, setting it behind him. Then he folded his hands on his crossed knee and smiled gently at her. "I would be delighted to do that for you. But, instead of taking your money, why don't we make a trade?"

This piqued Irene's interest. She removed her hands from beneath her and folded them across her chest. Her stomach still roared, but it was settling, anticipating.

"You come speak to me, just once or twice a month, for a dozen visits. Let me help you work through all that's happened. You can even bring in your friend as well."

She raised a brow. "That's all you want in payment?"

"Not payment. A trade. I didn't get a chance to see your uncle before he passed, and I owe him a lot. I feel that helping you would be a small part of what I owe. If you'll be a part of that journey with me."

Irene chewed the inside of her cheek again, this time making it bleed. This was her worry about visiting Doctor Roper sooner. She knew he was good friends with Uncle John and that he would've been at the funeral if she'd had more than six people there. And she should have visited him much sooner than this, even just for a personal visit. But he would've asked about her father and uncle, same as he did this time, and at no point until last year was she ready to speak about it. She knew she could say 'no' to his deal and he would still help her. But perhaps speaking to him wouldn't be so bad. She could chat about cases and keep him entertained for twelve sessions without having to dive into her own feelings.

"Deal," she said. "Once you've been to visit him, I shall sit down and bare my soul."

Roper chuckled and stuck out his hand. "I'm glad to hear it."

She shook his hand, then stood. "I shall give you Miss Hudson's number. Ring her before you go out. She knows Father's schedule and when it would be best to visit him. Also, thank you for all your help with the case as well. DI Lestrade will most likely be in touch about that culprit."

He handed her a small notepad to write on. "You caught him, did you?"

"Of course." She scribbled down her landlady's telephone number and right below it, her father's address. She paused as she finished writing, surprising herself with how easily she remembered the house number and street name.

"Excellent job. Take care, Irene. I shall contact you as soon as I've been out to see your father."

"Thank you, Doctor."

She left his office and a headache quickly crept across her temples.

* * * * *

Irene trudged up the stairs and entered the flat. Joe sat in his chair, dressed and well-rested, a cup of tea in his hand.

"Ah, there you are. Where did you go?"

She flopped on the couch, her hat tumbling to the floor. Isla pounced on it and dragged it to her bed.

"The hospital." She told him about her visit and the conclusion of Nettie and Lizzie. She held off mentioning her visit to Doctor Roper's, at least for now. Joe would praise her, and while Irene was always one for compliments about herself, her mind was still processing the thought of getting a professional assessment of her father and then having to speak to Roper.

"What about Annette?" Joe asked.

Irene undid the laces on her boots. "She did well, considering this was a very police-heavy case. We cannot pay her hourly, as we don't have anywhere to employ her. But perhaps on a case-by-case basis."

"She'll want a steady income, eventually. At least until she gets married."

Irene scoffed. "Another girl is going to be ruined by marriage."

Joe laughed. "She may choose to stay employed with us."

"She better. Or else I shall have some choice words for her future husband."

"Do you want to call her to tell her the good news?"

"Oh. Sure, I suppose."

"It will mean more coming from you."

"Why?"

Joe stood. "She idolises you. It's because of you, she is even considering this as a career. I'll go make you a cup of tea while you ring her."

Before he stepped into the hallway, Irene called to him. "Do you think we could actually do it?"

Joe paused at the door. "Do what?"

"Have an office and a business sign and an assistant and charge consulting fees properly."

They'd joked about it countless times before and Irene always brushed it off, but for some reason, now, the idea stuck with her.

"I don't see why not."

She bit her lip. "It does sound exhausting, doesn't it?"

Joe chuckled. "And what we do now isn't?"

She stood to pace and think. "It is. And what are we to do? Add running our own business on top of that?"

"Well, it would be easier, of course. Because all of our business stuff would be in an office."

"Would you still work at the vet practice?"

He shrugged. "Perhaps on occasion. Simply to keep my medical skills up to date, or to assist Michael on any surgeries that I find interesting."

"Hm."

Joe laughed again. "Let me make you a cup of tea. We can discuss the details over Christmas and just how we would go about even starting the business. Have a good, proper talk about it."

"Yes, good idea."

He left her with her thoughts and headed downstairs to Miss Hudson.

The business would have to be close to Baker Street. There was absolutely no way Irene would commute. And it would have to be close to a bakeshop or a wonderful restaurant.

She shook her head. All those thoughts could be left for later.

Right now, she was to ring Annette. She scooped up the receiver and dialled the number.

The young woman answered on the first ring. "Annette speaking."

"Hello, it's Irene."

"Oh, Irene! Thank you so much for letting me join to on that last case. It was exciting, dangerous, harrowing—"

"Yes, it truly was," Irene said flatly, then remembered that this was Annette's first case, and so to her, it probably was the most exciting thing she'd ever done. "We've dealt with better and more exciting cases, and I'm sure we will deal with more in the future. Anyway, I rang to see if you would want to assist in further cases. We'd pay you on a case-by-case basis and that wage is to be determined. It might be a last-minute call, as most times we cannot predict when a mystery will turn up at our door. And it wouldn't be all running and chasing bad men. Most of it would be paperwork and research."

At first, she thought the girl had hung up.

Then she heard a small sniffle.

"I would absolutely love that," Annette said, voice cracking. "I will make myself available whenever you need me. I get an allowance from my parents, and mend and alter clothes, so I am not desperate for money and will take whatever wage you offer."

Irene bit back a sigh. Her first lesson for Annette would be in the art of negotiation.

"Excellent. Once I discuss more with Joe, we will ring you back with more details."

"Okay! Thank you so much!"

She set the receiver down and sighed. Perhaps having their own proper private investigation business would reduce the need for police involvement, which would be ideal. As much as she loved Eddy, his rules did put a damper on certain things.

They'd have to come up with a company name, of course.

From her bed, Isla barked. She'd shaken Irene's hat and flung it beneath Joe's desk where she couldn't reach it.

Irene sighed. Perhaps she was getting ahead of herself. Christmas was only two months away. Once they got through the celebrations, then they could think of the future.

As Irene reached under the desk, Joe returned with two cups and a plate of biscuits balanced on top of one of the mugs. "Miss Hudson told me to only take two, but I took a handful. Come eat them before she notices."

Irene tossed the hat to the dog and hurried to him before swiping the plate of biscuits.

"Joe Watson!" A cry came from downstairs. "Did you take all those goodies?"

They both shoved a bunch of biscuits into their mouths, then caught each other's eyes. Joe laughed first, spraying crumbs all over the sofa. Irene followed suit, her chuckle turning into a cough, bits of biscuit flying all over the ground.

Isla was quick to react, slurping up the crumbs like a Hoover.

As Irene watched Joe attempt to chew his biscuits and keep Isla from eating all the crumbs, she realised it would take a lot of work to turn them both into the professional businessmen that they had pictured in their heads. So, perhaps after Christmas was best indeed.

Until then, she'd encourage Joe to steal all the biscuits he could.

The End

Holmes & Co. will return in:

The French Translator

A terrified man turns up at 221b insisting Irene and Joe take possession of a diary he is translating that was donated to the museum archives. The contents tell tales of murder, extortion, and other heinous crimes that this man wants no part of. Eager to seek out the author of this diary, the pair takes the book off his hands.

However, when a man from France finds them, claiming the diary belongs to his father, he asks the pair to find the person who donated the diary to the museum in the first place. Irene and Joe have no choice but to help, as he hails from a very dangerous family that could threaten the safety of not only Irene and Joe, but everyone who calls 221 Baker Street a safe place.

About the Author

Allison Osborne lives in Ontario, Canada with her son, their rabbits, and an overwhelming amount of vintage trinkets. When her mind isn't wandering through 1940s England, she's busy dabbling in scriptwriting and other grand adventures.

Connect with Allison:

Instagram: @allisonoauthor

Website: www.aosborneauthor.com

www.ingramcontent.com/pod-product-compliance
Ingram Content Group UK Ltd.
Pitfield, Milton Keynes, MK11 3LW, UK
UKHW020151020925
462463UK00006BA/86